First published in paperback by
Michael Terence Publishing in 2025
www.mtp.agency

ISBN 9781800949768

Cover design (AI)
Michael Terence Publishing

I would like to personally thank William Collins for giving me the initial breakthrough.

Contents

PART ONE

Introduction

An Ancestral Lineage

Geraldine has such a great interest, curiosity and fascination for her family tree, and those ancestors of theirs; and especially for Dorothy in particular - her ancestor. As a rule, Geraldine, an aristocratic granddaughter, didn't really talk about her ancestor to her friends, acquaintances, strangers, or to anyone else for that matter. Generally she kept it a personal matter. Geraldine normally confided in her family about it. To Geraldine, this personal matter was always private and confidential.

As always, Geraldine desired and wished to discover more about her great ancestor who had been deceased for centuries. On a sultry summer night, Geraldine stood looking at a gold-framed portrait of Dorothy on a wall in a dark room while she shone a torch on it. She saw the portrait when shining the torch light at it. Geraldine suppressed her tears. She wished to discover the secrets and strange background of her enigmatic ancestor. Geraldine also wished to learn and discover more about her ancestor - including about those who once deeply loved Dorothy, way back in the era of revolution.

1

Geraldine's Birthday Party

On Geraldine's birthday, her friends came to her home. At present, Geraldine was alone with her best friend, Ann, when suddenly her frantic brother entered the living room in an intrusive way.

"I know it's your birthday," he said. "Can you lend me some?"

Geraldine didn't answer her brother's demand. Thinking of his demand as a downright liberty, on her birthday in particular.

All of Geraldine's other friends were all together in the garden at this present time. Meanwhile, Ann stood still by a portrait and pointed at it,

"Isn't she an ancestor of yours?' she asked. Ann had asked this before, and was repeating herself.

"Yes, she is," Geraldine reminded her.

Geraldine and her brother, Charlie, came up to Ann who was admiring the portrait. There was other portraiture too, of their ancestral lineage. They all stood together and looked at a portrait of Dorothy on a dark background.

"That's Dorothy. She's far prettier than me, wouldn't you say?" groaned Geraldine.

"You look alike," remarked Ann, curiously.

"Do you think so? I do take that as a compliment," smiled Geraldine.

"She's family," said Charlie proudly.

A portrait hung on a wall opposite. A light reflected on it and it glimmered and shone. Meanwhile, outside from the garden, all of Geraldine's friends came back in doors.

Geraldine's mother called out to them, "It's ready!"

All of them came into the dining room. Some of them sat down at the dining table, sitting on dining chairs. The others stood around the dining table. Suddenly, Geraldine's mother came into the dining room and brought in a candle-lit birthday cake. She put it down on the dining table in front of her excitable daughter, who was sitting with the others around the mahogany table.

Ann stood behind Geraldine, and pressed her hand firmly on her close friend's shoulder. Her little brother, Charlie, smiled. Geraldine leaned forward. With strong puffs, Geraldine blew out all of the lit candles on the birthday cake. Geraldine made a wish. Today was Geraldine's sixteenth birthday - which was of coincidental significance.

Geraldine celebrated her birthday with her friends and members of her family. Only a few came to celebrate Geraldine's birthday. The few members of Geraldine's family, and her friends, saw how joyful, jolly and blissful Geraldine had been at her birthday party today. Today, this birthday of hers remains her happiest birthday ever! With the birthday celebration lasting less than an hour, truly it is a fabulous birthday memory of hers.

Geraldine's mother sliced up the birthday cake. She put a piece of cake on every red china plate. She gave everyone a slice of cake. Everyone was refreshed after some nourishment. Afterwards, Geraldine and everyone else came into the living room. This large room was spacious with a suite. Geraldine stood by a table. There on the table were Geraldine's birthday presents. She likes her gifts best of all. Geraldine felt proud of her friends. She loves them.

Geraldine expresses her thanks and appreciation, "Thank you all for your nice presents. Thank you so very much. Thanks for coming to my party today. You're all such a blessing! I really don't know what I would do without you all. I really don't! These gifts from you all are great. But there is something terribly missing from my life," admitted Geraldine.

"What's that?" interrupted Ann.

Geraldine stood in a still position. Her posture had the effect of making her look like a model. Geraldine felt her brother's hand on her shoulder. Geraldine felt deeply emotional at expressing her heartfelt sentiment.

"Dorothy, an ancestor of mine… I wish I knew her. I wish I could make her proud. I wish we all could," she blurted out.

Ann sympathised with her close friend. Her other friends and her brother were sympathetic too. These decent, good, and affectionate sympathisers showed their concerns, as well as their sympathy and condolence,

"Yes, we do understand. We all do," they said consolingly. "We do have you in our hearts. If there's anything we could do, we would."

Ann touched her friend affectionately.

"Dorothy is so dear to me," sobbed Geraldine, "she really is. I wish I knew her. I really do. I will always remember her."

Geraldine's tears ran down her cheeks. She cried, standing among her big group of friends and birthday guests, next to Charlie, her brother. Geraldine deeply remembered her ancestor with a tinge of sadness, and a fondness too. Geraldine did cherish her sweetest dream.

2

Geraldine's Past Memories of Her Family Photographs

On a cold winter weekend, a few of Geraldine's friends came to see their good friend at her nice, cosy home in a suburban neighbourhood. Geraldine's brother, Charlie, came into the spacious lounge with its new suite. At that moment, Charlie was being hospitable and talkative to his sister and her friends. Together they all had camaraderie and conversed together.

Unexpecting this at this time, Charlie immediately decided to leave the lounge. His unease caused him discomfort. He felt he had intruded on his beloved sister and her friends. Geraldine startled from her brother entering and then leaving the room. Geraldine rose from the leather armchair, and burst out of the lounge to stop her brother from leaving.

"Charlie, don't go. Stay with us. You don't have to go. Do stay with us," urged his sister.

Charlie smiled, acknowledging his sister's warmth and affection. Charlie declined his welcoming sister's invitation to come back into the lounge in the presence of her friends. In a split second, he had made his decision.

"No. I'll go, if you don't mind. You go back in," he hushed.

Geraldine respected her brother's decision. Geraldine left her brother to go back into the lounge, while he went up to his bedroom. Geraldine rejoined her three friends. She sat down on the settee with two of them. One friend sat cross-legged in a feminine way, and another friend sat at the corner of the settee, the position of her body at an angle. Stacey was elegant and graceful, and Rosie - a country girl at heart - was relaxed, reserved, laid-back and easy-going.

"Now, where was I?" stammered Geraldine.

"You got to the photos," Rosie reminded her.

"Did I? Oh! Yes! Now I remember! Let me see," said Geraldine. "When I was a child I did see photos of my family. They are old family photos. I don't think I have seen any photos of my ancestors - only portraits," she continued.

"That's a pity you haven't seen any," said Stacey.

Geraldine felt sad as she reminisced, "I guess it is," she admitted.

With languishing looks and frowns, both Stacey and Rosie expressed their deep concern for Geraldine. They disapproved of Geraldine's parents and family,

"It's a shame," said Stacey disapprovingly.

"Yes! A pity. You'll never know," said Rosie with concern.

Geraldine thought of her ancestral dreams, "I do think of my ancestors. I wish I knew them. I think of Dorothy. She's fascinating to me. I discovered she was once a milkmaid. Not those stories of a peasant," said Geraldine disappointedly.

"Never give up on Dorothy," agitated Stacey.

Geraldine admitted to feeling a closeness to her ancestor Dorothy and said, "I shan't! I will never!"

Geraldine did have a photographic memory of Dorothy, her ancestor. Geraldine became too deeply upset thinking about it. It did make Geraldine deeply sad, upset and tearful as she thought of Dorothy. Geraldine, of course, remembered her ancestors, and cherished and treasured her deepest ancestral dreams. At other instances, it was deeply upsetting, sad and heartbreaking for Geraldine.

As her friends consoled her, Geraldine stayed silent. She didn't blurt anything out, for instance. The archives and clippings; Geraldine kept quiet about in a secretive way. Geraldine *did* blurt out about her family tree, though. Geraldine focused on Dorothy - her main soft spot! Her voluptuous, fair ancestor! A buxom, country milkmaid. At this time, Geraldine intentionally didn't speak about anything else to her friends. Geraldine rested her head on a cushion. Suddenly, Geraldine dozed off as her friends talked away. In the far corner, by the wall, Geraldine rested herself in shade and shadow.

3

All Alone, Geraldine Marvels at a Portrait

One night, Geraldine found herself together with Charlie, her brother. Charlie was preoccupied with looking at his reflection as usual. Gerladine left her brother by going into another downstairs room (the reception room was being used). Geraldine walked to the side of the nearest wall. There she saw a portrait of Dorothy hanging up on the plain wall. Geraldine stood by the portrait. She admired it. This portrait was quite lovely, of a wild, natural, country, (mature) woman. Geraldine marvelled at it. Geraldine stood in the shadows. The big room was dark. Moonshine made a reflection in the shadows. Geraldine stood still for some time. Admiring a portrait of her ancestor. Marvelling at Dorothy's natural pose and poise. Her image portrayed a natural, childlike innocence. Dorothy had the look of an elegant lady. It's just an affected presence of her.

Suddenly, Geraldine started and jumped, as she felt her brother touch her shoulder blade.

"Well, what do you think of that?" asked Charlie, pointing to the portrait.

"Hey! It's quite something!" exclaimed Geraldine proudly.

Geraldine felt deeply emotional. Geraldine felt so proud of this portrait. As a result, now as Geraldine looked at it, it had a real effect on her and her emotions. All of a sudden, Charlie walked off, leaving his sister all alone again in the dark, moonlit room. Alone, Geraldine stood and admired the portrait further. She was lost in reverie. She had been spellbound by moonshine which made beams that reflected off the portrait itself.

Geraldine was enchanted by the shining moonlit glow. Geraldine stood by the portrait, glowing in a beam of moonshine. Geraldine was electrified by the glow, she was mesmerised by it. The enchanting moonlight illuminated the whole room, and the portrait, which was itself an object of illumination.

For Geraldine marvelled at a miracle. For actually, this created portrait materialised from a portraitist - not an artist.

4

A Day Out at a Seaside Town

Geraldine, aunt, uncle, niece and relatives spent a day at the seaside. They went to a pebble beach, and spent time together there. They sat down on deckchairs and enjoyed their time together. There they found it peaceful, tranquil, quiet and full of solitude. The family evoked a seaside nostalgia. But then came the intrusive tourists, holidaymakers, and sightseers to the pebble beach.

At once, the family left the beach to head to the promenade. They went to the shops and boutiques in the seaside town. They each bought a stick of rock - which of course is a seaside speciality and tradition - ice-cream, soft drinks, postcards, and souvenirs and mementos. They all liked their nice treats and knick-knacks. Sweltering in the sun, they all sat down on a bench. Everywhere were boutiques, shops, amusement arcades, cake shops, a fish and chip shop (another seaside tradition!), and a restaurant.

Geraldine liked her day out at the coastal seaside town. This nostalgic seaside town brought back childhood memories. Geraldine related to Dorothy, her ancestor. The day was reminiscent of Dorothy's visits to the seaside, and it was haunting. In the heat, sitting and relaxing on the bench, Geraldine stayed quiet as her relatives rambled on about the seaside again. Geraldine was ignored by her aunt, uncle and niece, as they all continued to converse with each other. Geraldine disliked them ignoring her. She took umbrage at them and how they ignored her. Subsequently, Geraldine spent all of her time with her relatives. Geraldine thought it would have been much better for her had her brother come today on the day trip to the seaside. Geraldine wished that was so! Geraldine had felt ambivalent towards her family, but she did like her relatives very much, in fact, at certain times, Geraldine preferred her relatives much more than anyone else. With the exception of Charlie, her younger brother, whom she loves too.

Finally they got back to the train station, to commute back to their county-cricket county. It ended up being a long, tiring journey home.

5

Geraldine Looks at a Wedding Photo Album

On a winter's day, Geraldine's mother left her daughter many family photographs on the top of a bureau. From an armchair, Geraldine got up after a rest. She came downstairs and entered the room where she would find the photographs where she expected to. Geraldine looked at her family photographs, realising as a result of it, that modern day Britain, society and times have changed. It's no longer the same as it used to be. These times are completely different. In today's modern society there is recession, depression, inflation and insurgency.

After Geraldine had looked at every photograph, she put the pile of pictures back down on the bureau. Something else took Geraldine's interest. Geraldine picked up a photo album. With curious interest, Geraldine looked through it. She saw wedding photographs of her relatives, they were in the Seychelles on a beautiful white beach, whining with bright golden lights on a dark night. Both husband and wife on their honeymoon. A married woman looks beautiful!

Geraldine thought of marriage herself - and a romantic honeymoon!

She wished she could escape herself. This ideal exotic location would be an escape to paradise - a tropical island of such beauty. Geraldine flicked through the wedding photo album. Geraldine saw photographs of romantic honeymooners on vacation in glamorous locations, ranging from tropical beaches and restaurants, to exotic bamboo thatched huts.

Geraldine took special notice of these romantic photographs - especially because her relatives looked like Dorothy. It was miraculous, in a way, at how much her relatives lived a life which Dorothy never could have. Geraldine remained confused and perplexed at how much circumstances could change. She couldn't quite fathom it.

This coincidental strangeness of everything did, in fact, result in a miracle of some sort. Geraldine resumed looking at the photos of the passionate honeymooners; of husbands and wives who had consummated their marriage and deep love in a sultry, tropical climate.

6

Geraldine's Brand New Shoes

On a nice Sunday afternoon, Geraldine spent time with her parents in the living room, which had some sort of Regency-style and mahogany furniture in it, with a fine, colourful Persian rug, and matching carpets. Geraldine relaxed by laying gracefully on a settee. In a state of unease and discomfort, Geraldine moved position on the settee, changing from laying down to a sitting up position. She glanced at her parents who were sitting in luxury leather armchairs on either side of her, with the intention of giving parental guidance to their daughter.

"Now, what can you tell me about Dorothy?" asked Geraldine.

"Ask your mother, she knows a lot more about it than me," replied her father.

"Mum? What more do you know about Dorothy?"

"My! Dear! Haven't we been through this before?" answered her mother impatiently. Her daughter had agitated her greatly.

"Mum! Tell me!" insisted Geraldine.

"Love, what do you want to know?"

"Dorothy married Mr Wendell. I really don't know much about it, do you? We are close to the Wendells, aren't we?" Geraldine asked.

"I don't know much about it myself," sighed her mother.

Geraldine put back on her slip-on shoes. She looked admiringly at her black leather shoes. Geraldine wore a shiny new pair of shoes. Simultaneously, mother and daughter got up, and went upstairs. Approaching the end of the landing, they came to a middle door that led to Geraldine's girlish, feminine bedroom. Geraldine and her mother walked towards a closet at the end of the double bedroom - the closet's lattice double doors already open. Geraldine pointed down to all her female footwear on the carpet at the bottom of the closet. Inside were many pairs of shoes; canvas shoes, boots, sandals, plimsolls, pumps, and trainers. Geraldine was obsessed with footwear. It was a traditional family trait and speciality of theirs. It runs in the family.

"Dear, it's so neat, so good," marvelled her mother admiringly.

Geraldine had a large collection of footwear - what lavishness and indulgence! Geraldine was proud of her footwear, naturally. All of her footwear was new or new-ish. The various materials were as follows: leather, suede, canvas, velvet etc. For Geraldine, only certain ones were her most favourite (the comfort of a pair of shoes are a personal choice!)

Geraldine's mother closed the closet doors. Her mother was houseproud and fussy. She liked everything to be clean, tidy, and neat. Geraldine's mother was obsessed with personal hygiene. It was an obsessive trait of hers.

Charlie came into his sister's bedroom. Charlie looked down at his sister's new pair of black leather shoes.

"Not another pair of shoes," he tutted.

Geraldine smiled proudly, "I'm afraid so," she retorted.

"At this rate you just won't have enough storage space left," pointed out their mother.

Geraldine became irritated by her constantly nagging mother, who did repeat herself.

"Tidy your wardrobe!"

"I will find some more, I always do," said Geraldine irritably.

"Huh! You do," smirked Charlie.

Geraldine became distracted as soon as her brother entered her bedroom uninvited. Geraldine looked down at her brother's plimsolls. These pumps were of an American-style design.

"I cannot see you wearing these much. I just can't. You don't really wear them," observed Geraldine.

"No, I don't wear them. I do wear other ones," replied her brother.

Geraldine bent down and pressed the front of a plimsoll, feeling for Charlie's toe,

"They can be tight, causing discomfort," she said knowingly.

Charlie acknowledged that he had that sort of complaint, "Yes they can. These ones I do wear. They are just right. A perfect fit, I must say so."

Geraldine expressed herself in her usual, common way, "I just don't wear a lot of them. They are just not right. It isn't a good fit," she said self-assuredly.

"Geraldine, you are assertive, that you are. You do make that clear," said her mother.

"Me! I am sure with experience I can make a reasonable judgement about it," expressed Geraldine self-confidently.

"A good fit is key. Not a bad one! The actual comfort of it is essential by the way, it shouldn't lacerate," said their mother assuredly.

Geraldine shook her head affirmatively. She did like to assert herself,

"Yes. If it does that, it's simply no good. With me it does not last long. I must go through stacks of them," she said.

"Honey, you sure do," smiled her mother.

Charlie looked at his narcissistic sister wearing her new pair of shoes, "Nice dress shoes," he remarked.

Geraldine stayed in her bedroom while her brother and mother left. Geraldine, feeling narcissistic, walked around her spacious bedroom admiring her new shoes. She suited herself and pleased herself. Geraldine stayed in her big bedroom, waiting for a friend to call at her house. As time passed by, Geraldine waited impatiently for her friend to call at her house. Suddenly the doorbell chimed. Geraldine hurried down the stairs to get to the front door ahead of anyone else. Quickly, Geraldine answered the front door. Geraldine welcomed and greeted her friend into her house. She accompanied the close friend into the lounge, leaving the door ajar.

Geraldine proudly showed off her shiny, new, black leather shoes with the gold buckle. An admirable sight was this beautiful pair of shoes.

"These are my dress shoes, what do you think? Huh?" Geraldine bowed.

"I really love them. They are lovely," exclaimed her friend.

"You're not wearing yours," said Geraldine, blinking.

"I am afraid not. It just isn't viable," replied her friend.

Geraldine and her best friend stayed together in the living room, spending time together amongst themselves. Thus keeping away from everybody else. Therefore they enjoyed a good time alone together. At this place, their privacy and solitude was a joyful delight!

7

Geraldine Talks About Dorothy

At home on a weekend, Geraldine was alone with her brother. Geraldine spoke to Charlie, her brother, about Dorothy. She received a negative response from her brother.

"It's all very well talking about Dorothy, but this is something that happened centuries ago. It's more like a tragedy, isn't it? - more than anything else. Dorothy was an orphan, a peasant. It is believed and rumoured that Dorothy, a young woman, wore such beautiful slippers one night. And a cobbler saw them. He fell in love with Dorothy. He proposed to Dorothy and they were wed. How amazing and magical. Then her life transformed for the better. It became a tale of rags to riches. A sort of fairytale. That's how I remember Dorothy. As I said before, it is a tragedy. Their marriage was a happy one, but unfortunately terrible things did happen. It is believed that Dorothy did have an affair. Her marriage turned sour. Then bad things started to happen to Dorothy. She had miseries, depression and desertion. Nothing got better.

Dorothy started to drink more and more. An alcoholic. Dorothy became suicidal. She was deserted by everyone. Bob was loyal to Dorothy. He always looked after Dororthy. He loved her. Even if Dorothy was depressed and abandoned by everyone. Then a misfortune. Dorothy ended by committing suicide by jumping off a cliff. How Dorothy did that, we do not know. It is a mystery," pondered her brother.

Geraldine was deeply saddened by Charlie's sad account of Dorothy, "You're quite right. Dorothy once lived the life of a princess, yes. It all ended up wrong in the end with Dorothy taking her own life," she affirmed. "Dorothy's husband, Mr Wendell, was a great cobbler. There was no one quite like him. A plump, eccentric little man with a *'Ho! Ho!'*"

"It is believed the cobbler worked with the elves," laughed Charlie.

"It could be. Is that some sort of folklore? I know things started to change. When Mr Wendell separated from his wife, he retired. He became a recluse in retirement, an eccentric," said Geraldine.

"It is believed that Mr Wendell went into hiding. He lived far away in the mountains and in his own cobbler's world. Making new shoes to suit himself. He made the best shoes ever. One of them being shoes or slippers he made for his wife," replied Charlie.

"What happened to Mr Wendell?" asked Geraldine.

"Goodness knows," said Charlie.

"Well, whatever happened, a company was established," said Geraldine.

"Yes, quite right."

Suddenly, their frantic, flustered, and frenzied parents entered the room. Both son and daughter immediately changed the subject. Talking about something else on this occasion. This time a light topic in the presence of their parents entering and coming towards them. Geraldine and Charlie still hadn't bothered to question their father about it. They noticed how calm, cool and collected their father acted at present. Their father had cooled off and calmed down. Both the son and daughter still hadn't questioned at all their father, for his intention and motive and objective. Neither of them had bothered to question their father about it. In a doubt, the brother and sister seemed unconcerned about it.

Simultaneously, both son and daughter rose. They left at once the shady, cool and shadowy room. Both of them forgot to mention it to their father. They had completely forgotten their minds.

8

The Shoe Children's Garden Tea Party

On a hot, sunny day during the summer, a group of children came to Geraldine's house. They all had been invited to a garden tea party at teatime. All of these children wore such fine, lovely shoes themselves. They were such good quality shoes. Geraldine knew these children well indeed. They grew up with Geraldine. Their parents were employees of shoe companies. Their families were friends of theirs.

Normally, Geraldine did prefer them much more than anybody else in preference. This is generally the case in this situation. Geraldine related to these children her pathos, empathy and ethics. The children's families worked for the shoe companies, and the shoe manufacturers' ideologies are the same more or less as others.

At present, all of the children invited to the garden tea party had stayed together in the lounge first before going out into the garden for a garden tea at teatime. All of those invited, including Geraldine herself, enjoyed the privilege of a garden tea party out in the lovely garden. It's a truly wonderful experience for them on a beautiful summer's day. The sunny weather was sweltering and a heatwave was scorching.

After the tea party had ended, all of them stayed out in the garden in a big group. Geraldine's mother and aunt cleared up the dirty and messy garden table by putting it all in refuse sacks, and then throwing it all in the outside dustbin.

Geraldine spoke to all of them. All of the children present at the garden tea party were: Steadman, Mills, Henry, Kath, and Miles.

"Kath, I like your shoes," remarked Geraldine. "You are cool. They are lovely."

"Well thank you. I like them. I like to store them in my shoe box. All wrapped up," said Kath fussily.

Geraldine then turned her attention to Steadman, "Steadman, I like yours. I really do. They are nice."

"They are not walking boots," replied Steadman.

"Mine are shoes with tassels on," pointed out Miles.

"Yes, I can see that. I really can. I do like it, it's such a nice style," smiled Geraldine.

"I am wearing black leather shoes. Not my hiking boots," said Henry proudly.

"I like them. Such nice shoes," remarked Geraldine.

"And may we ask, what are yours?" they asked Geraldine.

Keeping her balance, Geraldine stood somewhere in the middle of the enclosed garden, with its varnished wooden fence that surrounded it entirely. Geraldine felt happy and a natural joy, too. She looked down at her pair of slippers.

"Mine are a pair of black suede slippers, with a tinge of gold speckles on them. I do believe. Not sure," said Geraldine happily.

"Nice!" they exclaimed joyously.

Since the weekend Geraldine had been housebound as a helper and a host. Geraldine had been lumbered and personally responsible for some of the preparations for the organised tea party at teatime today.

Geraldine ended up leaving her house with all of the children on this sunny day. It's something which she hadn't intended at all. Geraldine went with all of them to a haunt of theirs later in the day. She had the initiative to actually stay in a frame of network at hers and at theirs.

9

Geraldine Looks at an Ancestral Portrait of an Ancestor

On a hot summer's day, Geraldine came into a room and went towards a wall. There at a wall opposite, she stood by a portrait hanging up high on the wall. Geraldine admired the portrait of Dorothy. A light gleamed and shone and reflected onto it. Marvelling at it, Geraldine saw Dorothy's visual purity. She admired her pureness. Naturally, Dorothy looked angelically beautiful. A pure angelic look of an urchin. Her lovely woman's face and countenance looked rather like the natural expression of a virgin.

Geraldine alone spent ages standing and looking at this portrait. It was a miracle how purely angelic it looked. It was so pure, like a virgin. Geraldine appeared to be mesmerised by this portrait. She stood for a long time, looking at and admiring it. Geraldine felt deeply emotional, tearful, and sad too. With all of her heart, Geraldine always remembered Dorothy (though other members of her family and extended family had feelings that differed from hers).

Suddenly, within a period of time, the room became dark. Geraldine could no longer see the portrait in the dark. Within time the whole entire room became pitch dark, and everywhere else as well.

Soon Geraldine lost interest in it. Quickly she walked out of the room. Leaving the door ajar. Geraldine didn't go back into this room until a few days later.

With a deep thought, Geraldine engaged in deep contemplation of Dorothy. With a deep love and respect she did revere Dorothy, her deceased ancestor. Geraldine wearied, and went into another room where she sat down in an armchair. She rested and closed her eyes. Suddenly she nodded off as she sat in the dimly lit room.

A few hours later, Geraldine awoke from her nap. Geraldine reached out and picked up her diary, which she had left on top of a sideboard yesterday. Geraldine wrote a brief entry in her personal diary:

If anyone should read this, be the first to know to have mercy for our ancestor, Dorothy. I remember Dorothy from the bottom of my heart. I regard Dorothy with such affection, love and respect. I still do remember her. I do know that my family won't!

10

Geraldine Goes to a Shoe Shop – Again (A Female Obsession of Hers!)

Geraldine went into a shoe shop, where she looked at various sections and departments in the retail chain, children's, men's and women's. Geraldine wanted to take a look and check out the latest trends and styles in all footwear generally. She spent time looking at various types of footwear in different materials. She saw on display various types of footwear: boots, slip-on shoes, lace-ups, plimsolls, pumps, sneakers, trainers, stilettos, canvas shoes, moccasins, walking and hiking boots.

Geraldine saw all the retail prices of all the footwear on display on the shoe shelves in the different sections. Geraldine thought this footwear varied in retail price according to quality and style. These were subject to and increased by VAT, according to inflation. Geraldine, a fussy customer, had spent most of her time looking at women's footwear. She liked stilettos and boots of all various styles and materials: suede, leather, and velvet. She also liked white cotton canvas shoes, which she took an interest and fancy to as well. She thought the general prices of these new leather boots were pretty expensive. She expected these prices to increase with inflation and according to the recession.

Geraldine obsessed over female footwear. It was an obsessive tendency of hers to go shopping of her own accord in shoe shops. She had an obsessional inclination to purchase women's shoes and boots. Her favourite colour was usually black. It was a normal colour choice of hers.

Geraldine sat down in a seating area in a designated section of the shoe shop. A luxury cushioned padded seating area. It was here the customer could try on new shoes. The fit is a perfect one. It fit nicely, softly cushioned, and comfortable on her beautiful small feet with padded cushioned soles. Geraldine was pleased with her brand new shoes. A satisfied customer who had pleased and suited herself. This pleased customer ended up buying a new pair of black shoes which filled her with natural pride.

She kept her new shoes on her feet. The sales assistant put Geraldine's old pair of soiled black plimsolls in a new shoe box, and followed by putting it in a new plastic bag. She had bought expensive shoes. Geraldine left the shoe shop feeling quite pleased and satisfied. A happy customer!

11

A Dream Night

On a weekend, Geraldine and her brother, Charlie, both stayed at their uncle's house. That pleasant Saturday evening, both brother and sister found themselves alone together in a big conservatory. They both sat down on garden wicker chairs. Leaning their backs against thick, soft cushions while facing each other in a parallel position. The conservatory plants were naturally lovely. Certain ones exotic and tropical, like rubber plants. The hardy ones, and evergreens, were being kept in the conservatory until they were ready to be put out in the beds and borders.

Geraldine and Charlie conversed with each other, despite there being differences and difficulties between them quite recently. But both brother and sister had made up by sorting out the differences between them.

Geraldine wondered as she began contemplating to forgive her brother, "Why is it, whenever I want to talk to you about Dorothy, you don't listen? Why is that?" she questioned.

"Look, it's not exactly a light thing to talk about," objected Charlie.

Geraldine questioned her brother about his grievance and displeasure. "Now, does it offend you? Are you embarrassed?" she groaned.

"This happened centuries ago. I do not want to talk about it. I have made that clear. But still you don't listen. None of you do," moaned her brother.

Geraldine looked languished, "You ought to show respect. We do know Dorothy wasn't an angel. She wasn't exactly decent. You know Dorothy had her faults. We all do. Don't hold it against Dorothy!" Geraldine was agitated.

Charlie flushed, "I try not to," he said.

"Dorothy may have been indecent and sad, but can you forgive? You mustn't hold it against her," insisted Geraldine.

Charlie admitted he did, showing his disgust and resentment against Dorothy, his ancestor.

"I dislike Dorothy's immorality. Her affair," he said disapprovingly.

"I do too. But you must forgive and forget. You really must. Where is that love in your heart for Dorothy? I can't see it, where has it gone?" asked Geraldine sternly.

"I do and I don't, if you know what I mean," answered her brother.

"You must buck up. You really must. For pity's sake," grumbled Geraldine.

Charlie, too, felt sad. With conviction he did feel deep grief. A sorrow.

"I should, shouldn't I?" mused Charlie. He changed his attitude. He did show sympathy to his ancestor, Dorothy. Does he still love her and remember her? Or is there still a hatred and resentment that he feels for Dorothy? Both emotional sympathisers should have love, reverence, respect and deep sympathy for Dorothy. Both had been tearful and so deeply sad as they poured out their hearts respectively. They both grieved for Dorothy. Their deep sorrow did cause them heartbreak. A heart-rending sadness. Especially Geraldine, who felt particularly heartbroken.

"That we will. We will remember her, we always will," she said mournfully.

"That we must. We shall always remember Dorothy deep in our hearts. Yes! Dorothy comes to us in our dreams," said Charlie sadly.

Geraldine felt bereaved and sorrowful, "I think she does," she said. "We must remember her."

Both brother and sister stayed together in the thick glass-paned conservatory until quite late at night. Eventually both of them went upstairs to the spare bedrooms to go to bed, late on this moonlit night. Did either of them dream of their ancestor when they both finally fell asleep, in their separate spare bedrooms?

12

Geraldine Alone at Home

Geraldine stayed alone indoors that day. Geraldine did not want to go out. Her unenthusiasm showed undoubtedly. She remained housebound and claustrophobic. With Geraldine being uncomfortable with the discomfort of claustrophobia, she kept away from her friends and people in general. Last week Geraldine did have problems, troubles, worries and anxieties. Also, a trouble-maker caused trouble too. Keeping calm and cool, Geraldine somehow solved every problem and trouble. She overcame her worries naturally. She no longer worried about anything. Geraldine knew people, individuals to be precise, and how terribly unfortunate they were, suffering from misfortune. These individuals were the unfortunate ones.

Geraldine was a believer, she had a good religious faith like that of a Christian. She depended on it for spiritual reasons to keep herself alive and well, as well as to survive life itself. Her personal faith was an important factor to her and to her life. She developed and grew a deep spirituality. Geraldine was deeply spiritual and religious.

Due to Geraldine's experiences, tragedies, and suffering, and from being deeply mournful and bereaved, she became naturally religious. Geraldine became rejuvenated, she regenerated, redeemed herself, and became enlightened and illuminated - it was a customary rule of hers.

Geraldine tended not to preach to anybody, as she deemed herself unfit and unsuitable to do so with any evangelism. Furthermore, it was against her principles. She kept her faith private. She did not want to give a sanctimonious impression to anybody, and at least she didn't impose her faith and beliefs to non-believers - unless of course it came to it due to circumstances beyond her control.

Geraldine naturally had a gentle and peaceful nature. She loved a story of peace. Nothing else could be better than that in broad and natural terms.

Again and again, Geraldine was alone at home, indoors in the study, sitting at a desk, with a pile of textbooks and a couple of encyclopedias. Geraldine was a bookworm. As a reader, she loved reading romances, she was obsessed with them as they were her favourites.

Later, Geraldine left the study after doing her studies. She went into the cool and quiet lounge. It was shadier there in the shadows at the back of the room. Geraldine sat down in the bright part of the room, which shone with natural light. She rested in a nice armchair. She relaxed and luxuriated in such comfort. During that time, Geraldine thought of her ancestor.

She reflected on her thoughts of Dorothy. She felt mournful thinking of Dorothy, her deceased ancestor. She tried to suppress her tears, but they ran; trickling down her rosy-peach, suntanned cheeks. Her ruddy complexion was Mediterranean, and she was a brunette. The expert application of a cream foundation meant she looked natural with make-up on her face, and her features looked naturally beautiful. It added to her natural look, giving her a lovely complexion - even though she was already naturally beautiful.

All alone, Geraldine stayed indoors. She rested and relaxed for the rest of the day. For Geraldine, having such considerable peace, silence, and freedom, was something to be cherished. She was free, with no restrictions imposed upon her. With no one (not even her beloved parents and family) intruding or imposing whatsoever. Whatever the situation, she was free. Therefore, she enjoyed her peace, quiet, and freedom. Geraldine did relish her freedom, peace, quiet, and silence. Geraldine felt a natural joy, she savoured her privacy and quietude. She wished it could last a long time, but how long for, she wondered.

The next week, Geraldine stayed overnight at a good friend's house in the suburbs. Geraldine valued and treasured good friendships - they were precious indeed. This, of course, personally meant so much to her. It was more important to her in essence than most things in general. Anything else was a secondary thing.

13

A Mystery Portrait (Hanging Up)

On a Thursday evening a few guests came to visit Geraldine's parents at her home. The welcomer showed them all around her house. Geraldine's mother was smug and houseproud. The visitors and guests looked in every room in the big house, and around the large garden too.

Geraldine expected the guests to enter the room. She anticipated their entry and arrival. At the wall opposite, there Geraldine stood, waiting for them to come in with her accommodating and hospitable mother. The few guests came into the large, spacious room, looking at the portraits on the walls. Looking at the wall, one of them was struck by the sight of a portrait with a dark background.

The curious visitor asked, "Who is she?"

Geraldine moved towards them. She stood in front of them, a few dilettantes and cosmopolitans - and her mother - all with good aesthetic taste.

"That one is an ancestor of ours," answered Geraldine proudly.

"It's really lovely," remarked the guest.

Geraldine actually tried to talk about it more to impress them. Geraldine was ignored by all of them provocatively, and her quick mother led them away somewhere else in the great house. Geraldine took umbrage at being ignored.

Geraldine stayed in the room, standing by the portrait of her ancestor. Geraldine admired, revered and marvelled at the portrait of her mysterious ancestor, Dorothy the mysterious seamstress. Geraldine sulked. She felt sad, mournful and tearful again. She wished she had known Dorothy. In her own way she loved Dorothy from the bottom of her heart. Geraldine deeply loved and was fond of Dorothy. Geraldine remembered Dorothy - an unforgettable memory of her. A deep remembrance of her beyond all question.

14

Geraldine Talks About Dorothy, Her Ancestor – Again

Geraldine, her brother Charlie, her mother, Kath, Steadman, and Charly, all sat outside on the terrace together. There it was sundrenched with radiant sun shining on it. The heat of the sun was far too hot. Geraldine tanned naturally, as she took her time to bask in the sun. Geraldine was decent at this time; her body mostly unexposed. The long sleeves of her blouse were rolled up, exposing her tanned arms. Geraldine had the tendency to be indecent at times. She was inclined to luxuriate in the garden and sunbathe for hours.

At present Geraldine wore a white, buttoned lace blouse with gold cuffs on the frilly sleeves, and a beautiful cotton, satin and silk black skirt with stockings and a new pair of calf-length boots, which were stylish and feminine. Geraldine was chic, stylish, elegant and lovely, all dressed up in her fashion in such a girlish, natural way.

They all sat in comfort out on the terrace. They each held a china saucer and a matching teacup in their hands. They each drank a teacupful of nice tea.

"Chances of our lives being like Dorothy's is quite slim for us. That won't happen. Will it? Not for us," groaned Geraldine.

"Who on earth can be like Dorothy? Not one of us. There was only one Dorothy. There is no one like her," said Charlie emphatically.

"I certainly do agree. Dorothy was destined for it. No one else really is. Are they?" murmured their mother.

Kath thought deeply about it, "Our destiny will never be like Dorothy, will it?" she mumbled.

The others, particularly the family, may well have been ambivalent towards Dorothy, their great ancestor. Geraldine loved Dorothy. She had always loved Dorothy, her ancestor. Naturally, her true feelings were different from the others. She was unashamed.

Geraldine concluded unashamedly, "Yes, Dorothy's life was tragic. That it was, yes, but Dorothyreached great heights. She achieved an accolade with her husband, an elfish cobbler whose dexterous and steady hands have a dexterity. Isn't the founder of an established company?"

They all praised Dorothy and her husband, a cobbler named Mr Wendell, in their own honourable way with a deep remembrance of them. They did regard them both with such great admiration (all of the children had a good admiration for Dorothy.)

At once they all stopped talking about Dorothy and her husband, the eccentric and conscientious cobbler from the past, centuries ago. All of them sat and sweltered in the heat. Perspiring and dehydrating in the hot sun. They all rose from their wicker garden chairs. They all went back inside to cool off in the shady, detached house. They all stayed indoors to suit themselves. Staying together or separately, they occupied rooms which were quieter, cooler and shadier. In these rooms they cooled themselves down. They felt coolest in the draught from the natural circulation. They occupied other rooms or shared the same room with others. Some of them wanted to be alone, individually. Others preferred being together, while the individuals liked to have their own privacy. Their wish and request was according to what they desired or fancied individually at that present time. From the scorcher today they had all got out of the hot shining sun. The hot, sunny weather was scorching and sweltering.

Within about an hour most of them had left the house to go home. They had all enjoyed their fabulous time together, out on the nice terrace on a lovely sunny day.

15

A Mystery Dream

Geraldine had gone to bed at her usual bedtime at night. During the course of the night, Geraldine just could not sleep at all. She twisted and turned in bed. Her continental quilt has fallen halfway off her bed. For Geraldine it was going to be another sleepless night. Geraldine sat up. She put on her dressing gown and slippers. She came downstairs, joining her relaxed brother in the lounge. That late at night, Charlie was watching a continental film on television at his own discretion. He was irritated at the intrusion of his sister's sudden presence. It made him moody and irritable, immediately realising his intrusive sister had intruded on him. This made him quite annoyed. Charlie lost interest in the adult film. It corrupted him, making him depraved, watching the torrid erotic scenes. Quickly using the remote control, he switched off the television set.

"Aren't you watching it?" asked his sister.

"Me? No! Not this time," replied Charlie.

"You shouldn't be watching that. Haven't we told you not to watch sex films?" said Geraldine discouragingly.

"Now what are you doing down here at this time of night?" Charlie wondered.

"I can't sleep," said his sister.

"Well that makes two of us."

Geraldine sat down in an armchair within reach of her brother, calming down when sitting close.

"You know, I can't sleep. I dream of Dorothy. It's really strange. Dorothy comes to me in my dreams. I can't understand it. I can't quite explain it. I can't describe it either. No matter how hard I try," confessed Geraldine.

"I dream of Dorothy too," admitted Charlie.

A philosophical Geraldine thought of a dream phenomena, "That's good. I dream too. So does mother."

"Does she? I wouldn't see that as being strange," said Charlie.

Geraldine had empathy and pathos, just like her mother did. She also didn't express her nightmarish dreams to anybody.

"I do have some empathy myself. That is without doubt I must add," grinned her brother.

Geraldien did share a paradise dream of Dorothy, her ancestor - a secret with her brother who seemed rather indifferent about it, more or less.

Geraldine was secretive when staying up late at night. She found it difficult to stay awake, but kept herself alert, in spite of feeling sleepy. After midnight, Geraldine and her calm, exuberant, relaxed and happy brother, both went upstairs to their bedrooms at the end of the landing, and at the bottom of a long corridor. There was a varnished oak bannister, and a staircase. Right at the top of it was another flight of stairs. They went to their respective bedrooms and got into their beds to go to sleep. Neither of them fell asleep until the early hours of the morning - at dawn to be precise! They didn't dream either.

16

A Country Summer

Geraldine and her family stayed at their family country retreat in the heart of the English countryside. The rural village was in a country that was quaint and idyllic, with a row of imposing stone cottages. As a result of them being intruders, they all made their way to the refurbished converted barn. At that time there were only a few of them, and they spent time talking among themselves. Geraldine experienced the story of the county - its beauty, nature and charm. Also, Geraldine found something there to her surprise and delight, which was Erica's fine collection of country teddies and cuddly toys. Geraldine admired how Erica collected teddy bears. Admiring them with a childish wonder. With admiration for it, Geraldine delighted with such charm, it was a whimsical sight of delight.

Geraldine thought of Erica as being childlike, with a childish nature of a child at heart. Geraldine marvelled at how beautiful the collection of country teddy bears was.

Geraldine, her brother, and their mother, stayed together and talked. Their father was away on a business trip for a few days. The family occupied a place, one room in particular, which was somewhere exotic and unusual in a renovated converted barn of such luxury. It was furnished and refurbished.

Charlie stayed silent as he listened to his sister and mother engage in a conversation about Dorothy. With an impatience, the intolerant daughter pressed her mother about her mysterious ancestor, Dorothy.

"Now, mum, tell me what you know about Dorothy. I insist you do. I must know more things I don't know about. I must learn and discover new things about our ancestor. It is my quest, and it's a discovery of ours which really needs to be made. For us to uncover it ourselves, surely for us, that is the case!" insisted Geraldine.

"Darling, what is it you want to know? You can tell me, love," said her mother affectionately.

"Why don't you start from the beginning. That would be a start," suggested Geraldine. Her mother remained silent. "Come on! Tell me!" Geraldine insisted.

Geraldine's mother looked deep in thought as she recalled and retraced as she spoke…

"Well, Dorothy was poor. She was an orphan I do believe - not totally sure myself. The orphans were taken care of at an orphanage, then another organisation. The years passed by. Dorothy was taken in by an institution. She went to a convent. It so happens that Dorothy loved shoes, she just did! She had a natural love for them. One day she wore beautiful slippers. It so happens that a cobbler saw them on her feet. He fell in love with her. He dated her. Then he proposed to Dorothy. In the future they got married. Dorothy was a married woman - the wife of a cobbler.

She became rich beyond her dreams. She lived her life to the full. She really did. Dorothy gained status, she achieved her goals by working in a shoe shop. Dorothy made friends with lots of children. They all loved her. She got on with them like a house on fire. Unfortunately, from there, things for Dorothy took a downward spiral and became a misfortune. It is rumoured and believed that Dorothy had an affair, and her marriage ended up on the rocks. As a result, all of the children who once loved her, deserted her - apart from Bob, who loved Dorothy.

Dorothy became an alcoholic. A heavy drinker. She suffered a miscarriage and from bouts of depression, misery and sadness. Dorothy ended up taking her own life as a result."

Geraldine appreciated her mother's account of her ancestor, "Now that's clear. I may have known that already. I do understand," she said appreciatively.

Geraldine felt deeply upset, and left both her mother and her brother alone together. She slowly went back to the retreat, where she ended up spending the rest of the day alone in a luxurious spare bedroom, thinking further of her deceased ancestor Dorothy.

17

Geraldine's Scrapbook

At the weekend Geraldine spent her time looking at a scrapbook. Her brother popped into a room and then at once came out of it. Charlie ended up doing something else, which previously, minutes earlier, he had been distracted from his mother by answering a phone call. The attentive son took the phone call, which he expected to receive. Charlie responded to the call he received.

A short time later Geraldine's mother came into the room to attend to her engrossed daughter, who had immersed herself in yet another distressing problem. A situation that was another girl's or teenager's story. Geraldine was deep in thought as she engaged herself in looking through ample notes made by certain children,.individuals whose eternal love for Dorothy was once deeply precious and forever. Their camaraderie was affectionate and emotional, joyful and a good one. There was also a passion and rapport, and everybody had a zest for each other's company and for being back together again.

Geraldine again felt deeply reflective and contemplative. She was lost in spiritual contemplation. Her reflection on the once glorious children was a joy and pride in itself.

"Mum, what else do you know about the children?" asked Geraldine.

"What you already know," her mother paused, "whatever has already been said. I've already stated the case as such."

Geraldine was losing her patience. She prompted her mother even more, "Mum, tell me anything you know."

"Well, sweetheart, Dorothy once bought a guy a new pair of lace-up shoes because his old ones had a hole, and the uppers were worn out. Another time, at Christmas, Dorothy bought some children new shoes because they were hard-up and miserable. Dorothy did treat these children to nice brand new shoes. This was Dorothy's way! She did it so well, with a finesse and style. Lacing up shoes and tying laces with panache. You shouldn't condole Dorothy in any way. You can't! You revere and thank Dorothy for her generosity."

"Yes! Dorothy was charitable and benevolent. That was her way! It's awfully good of her. Oh, I am jolly proud," said Geraldine joyously. Her mother *did* admire Dorothy, her ancestor.

"It is known that Dorothy gave donations to charity," said her mother admiringly.

With respect, awe and reverence, Geraldine admired her ancestor, "How marvellous!" she exclaimed.

"Just like good times," recalled her mother. "I guess at that time they must have lived in poverty - at least some of them."

Geraldine nodded knowingly; according to testimonies given and received, and testimonial sources and accounts of witnesses too. Without a question of a doubt, Geraldine made up her own mind. She was a humanitarian, that was definitely the case.

"Yes, it sure was," confirmed Geraldine.

Her mother choked back tears, "How awful! Those poor children!"

Geraldine, flicking through her scrapbook, did repeat herself, "Yes. It is. They are poor. That they are. It is all so bad."

Her tall, slender, bosomy mother got quite upset by it all. The unprovocative and elegant housewife rose and stood still, keeping her balance steady as she stood. Her poise and pose had all the secretarial elegance of a business woman in a conference room, or a plush suite in a luxury penthouse. Geraldine's mother sniffled. She blew her nose with a white tissue. She felt too distraught. It was all too upsetting for her to come to terms with. Too disturbing. She left her lovely daughter alone, quickly walking out of the room in quite an upset state.

18

Geraldine is Invited to Dinner with Lady Diners (Accompanied by Her Brother)

At an exotic beach restaurant, Geraldine dined out with other dinner guests (these invited guests are all loyal, devoted and dedicated employees of shoe companies.) They all wore lovely dress shoes and glamorous fashions that afternoon. Charlie wore a smart tuxedo and a new pair of black leather shoes. All of the glamorous, chic ladies wore glitzy evening dresses and black velvet or suede slippers. These lovely women were proud of themselves and their beautiful attire of evening wear from exclusive designer collections, as well as their dress slippers which gleamed in the light.

On this lovely celebratory occasion all of the celebrators celebrated. All of the chic ladies wore skimpy, slinky, fine fashion, as well as fine new footwear. All of the diners enjoyed a delicious savoury Mediterranean cuisine and a dessert, and drank fine beverages. The afternoon celebrations of merry-making and revelry ended up being the most memorable highlight of their time in this sultry, tropical climate, at an exotic beach paradise.

No individual took the limelight today; every diner was present here together at the exotic beach restaurant for this anniversary celebration, at this vocational location overseeing the exotic paradise island.

From that day on, Geraldine, a tourist and sightseer, never mentioned her wonderful and fabulous paradiscal experiences when on vacation to anybody. Though it still remained something deeply elusive and of a strange realm; wonderful and overwhelming and secretive to her, and perhaps to others.

Nowadays there was a constant bombardment and intrusion of retail commercialisation and European advertisement of both media and channel networks, as well as from international shoe companies. From a negative materialistic perspective, their prospects and minds are affected by a constant retail headache to try and utilise yet another seasonal sale. From the retail advertising and promotion of an exclusive, rural, outdoor footwear collection.

19

Geraldine Spends Time with Steadman

Geraldine took an opportunity to spend more time with Steadman, a playful grandson. Steadman's ancestor was known commonly as 'Bob.' Geraldine would normally spend about an hour with 'Nazi' Steadman, whenever she had the chance to meet him.

Both Geraldine and Steadman actually got on very well together, ever since their glorious former school days. He used a made-up, fictitious name to protect his identity, so he could remain unidentified with a certain anonymity. It was decent, acceptable and protective as a means of hiding and protecting his identity.

Meeting Steadman, people are inclined to be amused by his funny name. Finding it hilarious, Geraldine would laugh hysterically at his comical name. Others too, would be in hysterics. The name originated from the Nazi's, according to them.

Geraldine spoke to Steadman for quite a long time. She found him honest, sincere, reliable, trustworthy, thoughtful, and caring. These were the usually good qualities she looked for in a good friend. Of course there was no doubt, Geraldine confided in Steadman about personal, private and confidential matters. She could disclose to him without showing any fear, phobia, or anxiety - there were no imposed restrictions on what she could say, regardless.

Geraldine and Steadman had a good relationship and friendship between them. It was a close, admirable friendship and relationship. It was one that shouldn't be taken for granted.

When it was time for Steadman to go, he left Geraldine's home. Meanwhile, Geraldine stood by the top window, watching Steadman walk away down the pavement. As the season had changed, Geraldine had prepared food that included fresh lemon squirted onto big pieces of salmon that lay in a tin-foil baking tray.

20

Bob's Once Great Love for Dorothy

At present, Geraldine stayed alone in the living room, waiting for Steadman to enter. Geraldine waited and waited for Steadman to come, but at that time he hadn't yet. During the course of the day, Steadman, Kath, and Charly popped in to visit Geraldine's mother.

Finally, Steadman came into the living room. He was a few minutes late. Steadman made a simple apology for his delay. Steadman had got held up at a parking metre. Eventually he came in late to see Geraldine - a lady!

Geraldine, while waiting, sat still in her seat. She felt relieved when Steadman came in. Arriving late. The living room became cooler from the breeze and fresh air from thc opcn window. Geraldine showed affection, deep respect, and regard for Steadman. Her love for him was good.

"Your ancestor, Bob, loved Dorothy, didn't he?" sighed Geraldine.

"Bob really did love Dorothy, that he did!" replied Steadman.

Geraldine spoke up while staying seated gracefully in a velvet armchair. She took comfort from her position of sitting in a comfortable way.

"It's believed that Bob waited for Dorothy to show up about two times. But on both those occasions, Dorothy just didn't come. Bob was disappointed, but was tolerant of her as he usually was. He really was. He always did look out for Dorothy. He loved her. He really did. During those very last days of Dorothy's short life, most of the children whom Dorothy had loved had deserted her. Bob still cared. Only Bob really looked out for Dorothy. Bob had such love for Dorothy. Such a sweet love. With hope, Bob actually looked for Dorothy. He loved and cared for her. Nobody else had any love, concern, or mercy for Dorothy. Nobody! According to accounts by witnesses, I can confirm this is absolutely true," said Geraldine thoughtfully.

Steadman, standing in the shadows, was in a mournful state, so sad, sorrowful and bereaved.

"Yes! It is true! No comment!" said Steadman mournfully.

Suddenly Charly and Kath entered the living room to get Steadman, as they all intended to leave together. Quickly they left the house to get to the car parked in the drive. They hurried to get into the convertible (with its tinted roof rolled back), out on the drive.

Their long journey back home was a much better drive, to get back to their suburban homes.

21

Geraldine's Drawn Conclusion

Geraldine's brother, Charlie, left the occupied dining room (a few family members came out of the same room.) Geraldine stayed in here, sitting on a chair at the dining table (a set of antique dining chairs all around a big dining table. Everywhere else in the room were beautiful antiques, all of which added to the rest of the family antique collection. With a fine distinction, the distinctive furniture was the very best thing.

Geraldine resumed looking at a scrapbook of clippings. Her relaxed, cheerful, and restful mother was already there, sitting in an easy chair while reading her favourite women's magazine. At present, the irritated and irritable daughter, found herself intruded upon and disturbed from her reading by her mother.

"Listen, Mum! What else can you tell me about the children?" asked Geraldine irritably.

Her mother focused, "Not this again! Honey! What else do you want to know?" she asked patiently.

Geraldine expressed concern about the issue, "I want to know. To get a better understanding, I'd say to draw a better conclusion, naturally. Now why did they desert and abandon Dorothy? For what reason? What made them do so?" she questioned.

Her mother answered the question as best she could, struggling to find the truth and any real reasons.

"This all happened centuries ago. I believe the children's parents thought Dorothy was a bad influence, immoral, and sad. They did not allow them to see her anymore. None of them did. They grounded them from ever seeing Dorothy again. Dorothy must have been devastated by it. It would have been devastating for her! It would have made he so sad, heartbroken, and suicidal. Dorothy dreadfully missed those children. She loved them. She never got over it. She didn't recover - that was clearly the case at the time. Despite that though, Dorothy left a great legacy between her husband and herself," explained Geraldine's mother.

Geraldine was convinced of her drawn foregone conclusion. Finally Geraldine concluded,

"Let me explain. When Dorothy lost her 'great' job and had an affair, things just became worse for her. It all turned out wrong in the end. Dorothy turned to drink, and ended up having a miscarriage. Furthermore, all those she dearly loved abandoned and deserted her. Except for good old Bob, who remained loyal to Dorothy from the beginning until the last days of her life. Bob always cared for and looked out for Dorothy, always. Soon, Dorothy's marriage with her husband ended in divorce. Dorothy lost everything - including her reputation and her worldly materialism. Dorothy deteriorated; her life and her health too. Dorothy suffered from bouts of depression. A manic-depressive, suffering with melancholy and awful miseries.

For Dorothy, there was no doubt about it, she was sad and heartbroken. It was only a matter of time for Dorothy before she committed suicide. Dorothy ended up jumping off a cliff. What really happened that day, no one knows. It remains strange, a mystery," concluded Geraldine.

Geraldine closed her scrapbook for the final time that day. Dropping clippings on the carpet. Geraldine sat on the dining chair, while moving herself forward, and bent down to pick the clipping up from the plush carpet. She put it away with the rest of the clippings into her scrapbook.

22

The Female Theatre-Goers Go To a West End Theatre

Geraldine and a group of friends entered the entrance of a theatre in the West End. They went to the foyer. They saw a production of a mystery play. This long-awaited production of a suspenseful mystery by this cast was good (the previous theatre production wasn't quite such an all-star cast, as first reported by critics.)

These female theatre-goers were all interested in seeing this particular play, because they realised just how rife and common evil is, and that it was becoming prevalent in society today.

The elegant women took caution as a cautionary measure. Geraldine in particular, and her group of female friends, all looked ever so gorgeous tonight. They all wore such lovely dresses and quite beautiful footwear; black leather stiletto shoes, boots… as well as velvet or suede slippers of the same colour. All of them became overwhelmingly narcissistic at being dressed up and at how lovely they looked, this group on a typical girls' night out in the city near the embankment.

Their new footwear, especially, was their own personal choice of feminine female fashion, as were their really beautiful hairstyles and make-up, which accentuated their prettified and beautified features, and their natural complexions. It did actually make them all look naturally stunning, like fashion models!

In a group, these particular women were seen as provocative, ostentatious, pretentious, conceited and narcissistic, as well as too proud of themselves. A typical female characteristic may well be pride and narcissism - it is part of their make-up.

In the meantime, the other parties were arriving at an almost full-up theatre, and entering the crowded foyer. They were actually favoured ones from a concessionary group. They themselves had received a concession (a concessionary reduction followed by a discount for a group booking) for a party admission to the West End theatre.

All of them were being ogled, admired, loathed or envied… none of them quite the centre figure of glamour or focal attention as they hoped to be or dreamed of being. Suddenly, a busy and attractive usherette, shining a torch light into the pitch dark auditorium, led them to their seats in the middle row of an aisle. Everywhere in the full-up auditorium were theater-goers, seated and waiting for the play to start. The first scene's backdrop and background scenery was of a silent scene in a library.

After the first half of this theatre performance, the dramatics pause for an intermission. After the interval, the play immediately resumed. The intermission only lasted a short period. During the intermission, the group of women wearing jewellery, hats, gloves, and bandanas, joined the others going into a plush wine bar for a drink. The refreshments sated their appetite. All of the sudden, the beautiful, well-dressed ladies were standing together in a ceremonious way, in a big group in a circle, in the uncrowded wine bar. They suddenly heard the sound of a fuzz and buzz. Standing still they all listened to the clear sound of the tannoy. A clear instruction informing them of the commencement of the second half of the play. It was about to start any time shortly.

The audience didn't waste any time. All of them quickly got back to the auditorium and to their seats, slightly before the interval finished. Subsequently, the second half of the performance resumed.

In a full-house, the theatre-goers sat in the auditorium. All were enthralled and captivated. The audience enjoyed watching the gripping, suspenseful, well-acted, and dramatic mystery play. This nostalgic play somehow combined mystery with tragedy, and a tinge of tragicomedy.

All of them had a fine time that night. A truly romantic night with romantic notions. For all of them.

23

Geraldine's Account from Certain Friends of Dorothy (by Witnesses and Hearsay)

Geraldine stayed at home indoors. Wanting to have her privacy and be all alone. Sitting in her quiet bedroom near the window, she had her scrapbook on her lap. She was engaged in the deepest contemplation. It included the following: her deep spirituality, her worldly, materialistic desires, and her mourning for her ancestor. As usual, Geraldine mourned for Dorothy.

Geraldine reflected on Dorothy. Dorothy's life was a nostalgic era. From poverty to riches. An orphan from an orphanage and then taken into care. From being adopted by foster parents. Her new life as a young country woman trying to be an English country lady. An aristocrat.

Geraldine was deep in thought. She was fascinated by gentilities. In an obsessive way she has a fascination for it. From flicking through the scrapbook of hers, Geraldine already knew everything off by heart by now. She learnt and understood about most things, including bibliographical source material, archives, and clippings too. All of these things related to Dorothy, and anything concerning her.

Geraldine had some knowledge and understanding of Dorothy. She knew about her birth, her birthmark, and her birthplace, as well as her time at the orphanage, her adoption, and her marriage to her husband, Mr Wendell - a cobbler. She knew about Dorothy's dreams and her employment at a shoe shop. She knew about her obsession for footwear and jewels - jewellery was a girlish pursuit of hers.

Geraldine was aware of Dorothy's good relationships with her nice friends and acquaintances, and knew that Dorothy had been deeply fond of all the adorable and loveable children since she was a young country woman.

Suddenly Geraldine's mother burst into her daughter's bedroom. Geraldine stirred as she moved. She was startled by her mother's intrusion.

The stern mother pressed her daughter for an answer, "What can you tell me?"

Geraldine thought about it. She remembered what she had learnt by heart. Geraldine spoke about the main accounts, which had indeed moved and significantly touched her.

"A boy with no name," she said. "I shan't tell you his name or his identity. This boy said that Dorothy was kind, and that she bought him new shoes. Another one, a girl who had no money, said that Dorothy gave her money without expecting to get anything back. The girl said that Dorothy was the sweetest and kindest soul that she had ever known. This is an entry from a diary, I do believe: *'My shoes are worn out. My parents cannot afford to buy me any. Dorothy saved the day. She bought me new shoes. It was a treat from her. How lovely of her! She's a blessing to the orphanage.'*

"This entry is moving," continued Geraldine, "*'All of the girls had jewellery of some sort, apart from me. I was so upset and humiliated. Dorothy gave me a nice chain. I took it as a keepsake. I loved her for it. I shall always remember how sweet, kind, and sympathetic Dorothy was to me. Dorothy gives her stuff to charities. Not as a hand-me-down. This is something common she does from time to time. Dorothy is kind, benevolent, charitable and generous. When she goes to church she gives generous donations.'* And listen to this," Geraldine carried on, "this is another moving one; one night Dorothy accompanied her friend late at night. Why did she do that? No one else would really make an effort to do so, listen: *'Dorothy risked her own life by walking with me in the middle of the night in the dark, and then walking back home. Why Dorothy did that, I just don't know. Who on earth would do such a thing for me? It's amazing! How I love her for what she did. Dorothy gave me some money too, how nice of her!'* Dorothy did charity work and events that were not publicised. She helped out at summer fetes and jumble sales held at grounds and church halls, as well as doing bric-a-brac - a sort of child's speciality of hers. Dorothy let Bob down at times, but she made it up to him by treating him to new pairs of boots."

Geraldine kept the rest quiet, but she mentioned other things to her mother, who was deeply upset and mournful after hearing these accounts, and insisted her daughter stop blurting things out.

Geraldine obeyed and grew silent. Her mother left her bedroom, going back downstairs to join her sister. Meanwhile, in her bedroom, Geraldine sulked and sobbed. She felt deeply upset, sad, sorrowful and bereaved. Geraldine was coming to terms with the reality of discovering her descendant's past and history.

24

The Deep Fascination of the Portraiture

Guests visited Gerlaldine's uncle's country manor. The groups were well entertained, playing chequers and rumi while a few of them drank whiskey. They talked about business, and had a country tea out in the lovely manor house garden. They enjoyed the delightful treat of having a country garden tea on such a lovely summer's day. The hot, sunny weather was sweltering. It became hotter and hotter during mid-afternoon and during the course of the day.

They sat on garden chairs at the table. They heard the sound of running and flowing water from the garden fountain, with its powerful water-jets emanating from it. In the light the crystal water glistened. The sound was of flowing, pure water. A pure source running.

Geraldine anticipated them coming back into the country manor house. She stood and waited for them in a large room with antiques. Geraldine stood at the far end by a wall with a high skirting board. She stood in front of the portrait hanging on the opposite wall. The guests all stood together and looked at the portraiture on the walls. They saw a portrait of a descendant and ancestor. One of them in particular took interest in it. Spontaneously it appealed to all of them from first impressions. Did they marvel and admire it, or was it just something of an acquired taste?

They each made a remark about this portrait, and one simply commented on its instant and immediate appeal. Geraldine ended up standing still in the exact same spot she always did when looking at the portrait of her ancestor for such a long time. For Geraldine time and her existence seemed to elapse, and she became a non-entity. By that time all of the guests had already gone. The drivers had taken their passengers off in their vintage cars or convertibles, and driven them back to their homes in Kent.

25

Geraldine's Deep Sympathy for Her Descendant

Geraldine made lots of notes during the course of her research, from the archives and from reading up on it. Geraldine learned and discovered new things. From witness accounts she found out that her ancestor once had aspirations to work in a shoe shop. Ultimately this dream of Dorothy's became a reality. Dorothy ended up working in a shoe shop courtesy of her husband, Mr Wendell. Overall, Dorothy's best days were once in retail, employed and working in a shoe shop for a few years as a part-time sales assistant. She served and attended to customers as well as replenished the stock in the stock room. Due to circumstances beyond her control, Dorothy had to give up this position and her short-lived career, due to risks and dangers she could not quite cope or deal with, as well as her stressful working conditions, responsibilities, and her regular routine.

Dorothy resorted to being a housewife. Of course it was something that came naturally to Dorothy, and she did it well. Dorothy made many friends. Some of her friends were children, whom she loved very much. She adored them, these loveable children. Dorothy was deeply fond of them. (Dorothy's other friends and acquaintances were adults, heirs, employers and employees.)

At times, Dorothy would treat the children to footwear whenever it was required. Dorothy provided them with many types of footwear. Of course, naturally, the children preferred their favourites. They each certainly made that clear when expressing their thanks and gratitude. Dorothy looked after them like her friends in the orphanage. Dorothy would cry when she thought of her past, of her deep love and fondness for the children that brought her such rapture and joy.

How long would her friendships and acquaintances last under these circumstances? Consequently, as a result, there were ill-fated changes to Dorothy's life. Her misfortune, and her unfortunate self-destruction. Dorothy never recovered from it, and committing suicide was imminent. It was predictable what would ultimately happen to Dorothy, ultimately at any time of her ill-fated life. A misfortune and tragedy which ended up being inescapable and unavoidable for Dorothy.

Dorothy was obsessional about shoes, slippers and ankle boots - especially new leather ones. She obsessed over her favourites. She was obsessed with footwear; she did have a female obsession for it. This obsession was a stylish, feminine trait of hers.

Eventually, when Dorothy lost her job, everything seemed to change for the worst. Ultimately she suffered misfortune and self-destruction, a decline in morals and morality - a complete disregard for it! She started to please only herself, with an unrestrained nature. For her this was a wild decadence! Perhaps even self-indulgence. She began to disregard decency and engage in indecency. Dorothy's affair led to a miscarriage, divorce, alcoholism, addiction, desertion and abandonment - all of which caused Dorothy to commit suicide in the end.

Geraldine was lost in deep thought. Geraldine sympathised with Dorothy. She mourned for her, her ancestor and descendant, with a sympathiser's sympathy.

26

Geraldine Talks to Her Brother About Dorothy, Their Descendant

On a Saturday winter evening, Geraldine and her brother stayed indoors together at their home. Their parents had gone away on a weekend break. Geraldine and Charlie both warmed up from the central heating. From room temperature it increasingly became warmer. Indoors was insulated from the double-glazing.

Geraldine luxuriated in a position, lying across the settee in a graceful way. Charlie sat in an armchair in the corner, close to his sister who luxuriated in a graceful fashion, her figure like a sylph's.

"It's just us," smiled Geraldine

"Yeah, it's great. It's only us," grinned Charlie

Geraldine relaxed, comfortable and lackadaisical, as well as deep in thought, moved her body to change position again.

"I was thinking of Dorothy. Why did she have to die so young?" said Geraldine.

"Not this again! What is it this time?" muttered Charlie.

Geraldine, deep in her mind, dwelled upon when Dorothy had lived in the orphanage.

"Dorothy was unhappy. She spent years living in an orphanage. She made friends, and they all hoped that one day they would get adopted. But it just wasn't the case. Eventually, certain children *did* leave the orphanage, finding themselves adopted, but the majority ended up living at the orphanage day after day, year after year. Dorothy liked her friends. She made good friends. But the relationships didn't last once one of them left the orphanage. Shelley was adopted - Dorothy wasn't! Neither were any of her friends.

Dorothy had a religious upbringing. She didn't quite believe a non-believer. She did say her prayers, asking God to forgive her. Dorothy's friendships were good ones, she was attached to a certain few individuals. Unfortunately for Dorothy, a good friend of hers left the orphanage, and this must have made her devastated. Miserable and unhappy, Dorothy clung to her ideals. She prayed, wishing and hoping for better things to come into her life. Dorothy spent days sewing and doing needlework, cooking, cleaning and washing. On other days, going out with her friends to the golden fields - to her a place of dreams! Dorothy went out on nice outings and day trips, too. Finally, Dorothy's life changed. Dorothy was adopted. She was relieved to have left the orphanage. Dorothy missed her orphan friends. Dorothy ended up living in a lovely house in the country with lovely foster parents. Her life changed for the better. Dorothy was really happy. She could not believe her fortune at all. She just could not!

Dorothy was loved, cared for and pampered by her adoptive parents. It was an unbelievable transformation of her life. Dorothy loved her foster parents. She did gain a sense of purpose in her new life, with all the freedom and free will. Dorothy developed a good, loving relationship with her foster parents. They pampered Dorothy, and she depended on them. It is believed that Dorothy entered a convent at some point, and was there for many years. I don't know. Did she really know the implications of a Catholic religion? Going into that institution, Dorothy became benighted and bedevilled. Leaving the convent, she became withdrawn, unhappy, disconnected, and possessed. When she did finally see the late, it must have been far too late.

Growing up as a young woman, Dorothy had a flair for fashion and style. She dressed up and wore fine shoes. One day, Dorothy got her lovely pair of shoes shined, and instantly, the cobbler doing the shoe-shine fell in love with Dorothy. The cobbler dated Dorothy. The couple became betrothed and got wed. The wedding of theirs was a cobbler's one, with all of the guests wearing new shoes. Their Scandinavian honeymoon was a Danish one. Dorothy's marriage was happy and romantic. Dorothy worked for her husband the cobbler, then ended up pursuing her dream of working in a shoe shop. Dorothy befriended children, and they really loved her. Dorothy advised them and was fond of them. When Dorothy lost her job, she was badly devastated by it. She never really recovered. For Dorothy, things in life started to go really bad. She began to lack morals, principles and integrity. She became tempted, materialistic, greedy, worldly, and decadent. It so happens that in the end Dorothy ended up having a fling and an affair.

Then Dorothy had a miscarriage. Her marriage was on the rocks. Mr Wendell separated from his wife and ended up serving her with divorce. Living alone, abandoned, Dorothy became deeply unhappy and suicidal following a drinking problem. In a flash, all her friends, and the children too, had deserted Dorothy. Only a true friend, Bob, truly looked after Dorothy in the end, as the story goes.

But her death… was it a cover-up? Was Dorothy drunk? In despair, and feeling suicidal, she ended up taking her own life. It is believed she may have been drunk and jumped from the top of a cliff. As a tribute, all the mourners wore black armbands and new shoes (which the cobbler had made for them), as a mark of respect for Dorothy."

Charlie had listened to his mournful and emotional sister express herself and explain by giving an account of Dorothy's sweet, short, and tragic life. The glamorous lifestyle of a cobbler's wife. Dorothy left a great legacy behind.

27

Lost in a Trance

One a cold midwinter night, both Geraldine and her brother found themselves at home together. Neither of them had gone out, even though it was a Friday, instead they both ended up staying indoors. The house was warm and cosy, every room warmed from the central heating. They both took comfort from the warmth and the rising temperature. Geraldine luxuriated in comfort, lying across the settee in a supine position, her head resting on the cushioned armrest. Her brother sat in an armchair, set at an angle in the far corner, near to his sister. In a lackadaisical and day-dreamy way, they felt relaxed, restful and lethargic, yet cheerful. Both brother and sister enjoyed their time alone together. They had a good brother/sister relationship; intimate and close.

Geraldine and Charlie lounged together, resting in silence. They glanced at each other. Geraldine giggled and her brother laughed. Theirs was a childish, hysterical laugh. Their laughter echoed throughout the wooden-beamed, tudor-style room. Simultaneously brother and sister stood up. They preened and smartened themselves. Geraldine and Charlie went into another spacious room, and approached the opposite wall. Portraiture hung on the wall directly in front of them. Standing together side-by-side, Geraldine and

Charlie stood by a portrait. They both felt proud as they greatly admired the portrait of their ancestor. It was the sight of natural blondeness; Dorothy's fair hair, so shiny and beautiful. In the light her blonde hair shone with brilliance. It really was a sight of such beautiful blondeness.

Both Geraldine and Charlie were saddened at the sight of a portrait of Dorothy. It upset them and made them so sad. Both brother and sister mourned for Dorothy, both of them deeply mournful again. It was far too upsetting for them, looking at the portrait. They looked at it for a long period in silence.

Standing still, Geraldine was sad and tearful. She was overwhelmed with deep sorrow. Her tears ran down her cheek. Her naturally high cheekbones which were beautifully powdered with foundation and applied with rouge from her compact. Her natural complexion required little make-up or creams. She had the beautiful complexion of a natural blonde.

From this unusual situation of being alone together late at night, both brother and sister were deeply saddened and mournful. They must have stood by that portrait for at least an hour, which seemed to them like many minutes of time passing by - oh how time elapsed! Time actually stood still on that long winter night. Geraldine's ladies watch fast, and her brother's wrist watch slow.

28

Geraldine's Trance and Reverie

Geraldine, during the course of the day, did stay at home, waiting for a close friend to come round. A good one! Charlie came into the lounge. He intruded on them. His hands were oily and greasy, holding a cloth with stains on it.

"Are you going to join us?" asked Geraldine.

"No. I am going back out to the shed to help Father repair a puncture on my bike," he answered.

As soon as Charlie left the room, Geraldine and her friend, Lily, resumed talking.

Lily rested her chin on her palm, "Now, where were we?" Lily paused. "When I leave, what are you going to do today?"

Geraldine thought of her plans. She intended to pursue a purposeful objective of hers!

"I am going to try and find out more about my ancestor," replied Geraldine.

Lily raised a pointed finger, "Well, haven't you done that already?"

"Oh no! I haven't. I am always learning something new."

"What else will you find out?" enquired Lily.

"I am trying to find out more about Dorothy's marriage. I would like to know more about her good relationships with children. Dorothy also had such style, flair and panache with all types of footwear. It was a speciality of hers. Mr Wendell and his wife were two of a kind!" responded Geraldine assertively.

Lily pondered thoughtfully, "Now that is interesting. It really is. You ought to know most things by now. Or at least have some sort of gist of it," she said confidently.

"That I must," said Geraldine.

"You look like Dorothy," remarked Lily.

"Do I? Do I really?" shrugged Geraldine.

"Yes. You do. I wouldn't be saying it otherwise," retorted Lily.

Geraldine thought about it deeply. Geraldine's resemblance to Dorothy made her feel proud, naturally. She already knew she looked like her ancestor. It made her feel proud and joyful. Geraldine was pleased by Lily's compliment.

"I am glad you think so. Others think that too," said Geraldine proudly.

"Despite what people think, you should be proud of your ancestor, you really must," said Lily unashamedly.

"Yes, you're right. I should," agreed Geraldine.

Both Geraldine and Lily got up from their seats simultaneously. They both left the lounge and went into another large room. Geraldine and Lily walked together to the far wall. They stood together by the portrait hanging up. This portrait stood out compared to all the others hanging on the walls. Geraldine and Lily stood together and looked at the portrait of Dorothy. They both admired the portrait, marvelling at Dorothy's beauty and fairness, her countenance, poise, pose, elegance and grace. Meanwhile, Geraldine stood still by the portrait for such a long time. She ended up becoming lost in a trance, a deep one, and also a reverie. Geraldine has even been unaware that Lily had left and walked home, leaving Geraldine all alone.

29

A Historical Revelation About the Norwich, Norfolk, and Northampton Children

Afterwards, Geraldine stayed for a long time in her bedroom. Geraldine then decided to go downstairs, where she rejoined her aunt, brother, and mother. At present, the family were spending time talking. Geraldine sat down in an armchair. She slipped her slippers off her small feet, and rested them on a footstool in a comfortable way. Geraldine glanced sideways at her aunt, who was sitting next to her brother Charlie, and her mother, on a velvet settee.

"As a matter of interest, do you know anything about the Norwich 9?" enquired Geraldine.

"Are you referring to the group?" questioned her aunt.

"Yes. To be precise, the children themselves," replied Geraldine.

"Dear, you should ask your mother. She knows far more about it than I do," said her aunt.

"Mum, do you know anything about the Norwich 9?" asked Geraldine.

"Yes, I do. Haven't we been through this before?" frowned her mother.

Geraldine repeated herself, "Do you know anything about the Norwich group?"

"What's that?" interjected Charlie.

His aunt ignored him, but answered the question, "These were the ones who became professional. At the time they may have been children that Dorothy was fond of. She loved them all. Their parents worked for shoe shops, shoe companies and in distribution. I do believe the children followed suit. All of the Norwich ones were great professionals. They were commended and noted for their professionalism. They themselves were the hallmark of the company's brand," explained their aunt.

Geraldine recalled the notes she had made.

"They worked for Dorothy and her husband," she remembered.

"Yes, they did. They were a great team. They were certainly that. In the end, a few of them became alienated by it all. They left the group, team and company. They ended up working somewhere else," answered Geraldine's aunt.

"Oh! What a shame! When they left, it was never quite the same again. It failed to capture its former glory and success," Geraldine pondered.

"I should say so," murmured her aunt.

"That's a disappointment," commented Geraldine's mother.

"So what happened to them?" asked Geraldine.

"Well, they left them. If I understand it right, Dorothy was deserted by all of them. Except for Bob, who loved Dorothy."

Thinking about it, Geraldine was saddened. It deeply hurt her feelings. It made her feel ever so sad.

"What a pity. That must have been the end."

With some knowledge, Geraldine's mother knew, "In some ways it was the end," she said. "They never ever gained the great success they had once attained and were renowned for."

Geraldine had learnt the truth. But she was simply undiscovering new things - for she already knew these things by heart.

Geraldine felt deeply upset again, then at once took her feet off the pouffe. She sat up and rudely hurried out of the room in an unladylike fashion. Geraldine kept away from her family for the rest of the day. Reaching her bedroom, Geraldine quickly locked her bedroom door. She threw herself on her bed and wept.

The following afternoon, Geraldine spent some leisure time with a group of friends in some local gardens, within proximity of the high street. Afterwards, one of

Geraldine's friend's parents dropped her home. Back home, Geraldine relaxed, then spent time reading the notes in her scrapbook:

'According to a witness, at a summer fete, held on a nice green, Dorothy and certain children were helping out. Everyone got involved in doing something. Bob did the cleaning up of a marquee and stacked up chairs. Dorothy helped out at the jumble sale. Another girl helped out with bric-a-brac. Tommy helped with the raffle. Another person helped out with giving out the prizes to the winners, for example, a teddy bear or a goldfish. Another helped out on the sweet stall. A confectionary with toffee apples, black-jacks, sherberts, candy and liquorice. A chubby boy helped out with pin-the-tail-on-the-donkey, and finally, last but not least, someone else was on the lucky dip.

Everyone worked hard on that long day at the summer fete. The sounds were crowded with the general public who were visiting. Everyone had worked hard, they had been charitable and benevolent while serving and attending, and it had been a self-satisfying, enjoyable and rewarding undertaking. It all ended on a high. Finally, before it was time for them to go, they all gathered together to get their picture taken.'

30

Geraldine's Introspection and Reflection on Her Ancestor

After Geraldine had taken an afternoon nap, she left her bedroom and came downstairs. Geraldine came into the living room, where she sat down with her brother, who was reading a comic.

"You're not reading that," said Geraldine hoarsely

"Why shouldn't I?"

"Are you working today?" asked Geraldine.

"No, not me. How about you? You're not working, are you? You're a lady of leisure, aren't you?" replied her brother.

With no shame Geraldine admitted, "Yes, indeed I am. That, by the way, will soon change. By this coming summer I shall be working abroad on a pirate ship," she smiled.

"You are? How nice. Are you still reading up on Greek mythology?" asked Charlie.

"That I am. My friend, Gill, works for a travel agent, and *her* friend works for a tour operator," blurted out Geraldine.

"What on earth are you going to do today?" her brother asked.

"Well, I am going to spend my time finding out more about my ancestor," answered Geraldine.

"OURS!" Charlie reminded her. "Well that's good. I'm glad you are. Really someone in our family should. You know it's something of an obligation."

"Quite right," said Geraldine sullenly.

Charlie pressed his sister on her findings, "Have you found out any more about Dorothy yet?"

"That's a good question. I am trying to find out how Dorothy must have felt. But I've only drawn my own conclusions on the matter so far," Geraldine paused. "Dorothy lived a glamorous high-life. An over-indulgent and self-indulgent one too. Dorothy was generous and benevolent. It was in her nature. Things in her life turned sour and terribly wrong. It just did. Dorothy lost her morals; they just declined. Dorothy ended up having an affair. Then, much later in her life, she had a miscarriage. From then on, Dorothy knew it was the end of her marriage. She realised the harsh reality of life. The ones whom she dearly loved all deserted her. Apart from Bob, who stuck by her and looked out for her, always.

Dorothy felt unloved, miserable, sad and suicidal at living alone. Her separation from her husband took its toll. She had a drinking problem. She became lonely and withdrawn from everybody, and from society. The things Dorothy took for granted were longer at her disposal. Dorothy lost everything. Absolutely everything. She was in a suicidal state. Dorothy ended up taking her own life. It was inevitable. Dorothy left a great legacy behind with her husband," Geraldine finished proudly.

Charlie clasped his hands together, "Oh, she did!" he exclaimed proudly.

"We are so proud of our Dorothy," said Geraldine.

Suddenly, Geraldine and her brother stood up. They left the room together at once. Geraldine and Charlie went into another room; a grand and stately room with fine and beautiful antiques in it.

Both Geraldine and Charlie walked towards the other side of the room. They came to a plain, white, shadowy wall with reflection on it. They stood opposite it, standing together to admire and marvel at the portrait of Dorothy, their great ancestor. They spent a long time together admiring, marvelling and looking at the portrait there in the dark, shadowy, moonlit room.

31

Geraldine and Her Brother's Sorrow

In the cool and shady study, Geraldine sat on a swivel chair at the desk with the lamp on. She studied the notes she had made, referring to her scrapbook in certain cases. Charlie entered the study, he stood in front of the desk with his arms folded. He stood in front of his seated, studious sister. Geraldine explained that she intended to make clear Dorothy's ideals.

"Dorothy was bloody miserable at being poor. She wanted to get a better life. She desired it. She wanted to get out of the orphanage. She often dreamt of a better life for herself. She had fantasies and dreams. She was a romantic person. Her fantasies and dreams meant so much to her, they really did. They were all she had during those hard times. Dorothy loved her friends too. She missed all of them when she left the orphanage and was adopted. I don't think she ever saw them again. From that time on, her fortune changed for the better. It certainly did. Did Dorothy then go to a convent? - Dorothy wasn't really a practicing Catholic, like she was supposed to be from her Catholic upbringing. Far from it. At that time, for her, it would have been a tall order.

Dorothy loved fashion. She had style. She loved footwear too. She changed her hairstyle from time to time too - that was a trait of hers. There was no doubt that Dorothy was disturbed. That she was. As a result of her new, adopted life. Dorothy loved rural country life, and her country lifestyle. She had lots of freedom to do whatever she wanted. Her ideals never changed, they just stayed the same. She did indulge in pleasure - that was one thing she did do! Dorothy had such class! Maybe she was vulgarian? With her peasant's background… a plebian! Dorothy was a typical romantic woman who loved romance and glamour. A herbalist too, who had great flower arranging skills and green fingers.

Her life changed again when one day, she had her shoes shined. That day, the cobbler and Dorothy fell in love. Then they dated in true Scandinavian fashion. Dorothy and Mr Wendell ended up getting married. She was a truly happy wife. Dorothy's life changed from rags to riches. She worked with her husband, assisting him in his workshop - an assistant to a cobbler. Dorothy ended up working with her husband for years. During that time she made good friends within the community. Dorothy was loved by all of the children. They always looked up to her. As a result of all her success, triumph, and love of the children, these were the best days of Dorothy's life. The rest of it is history. For Dorothy, it all turned out wrong in the end. A tragic misfortune. A tragedy," said Geraldine articulately.

Charlie had listened intently to his sister, clearly understanding. He was interested and concerned about hearing Geraldine talk about their ancestor. He felt upset, sad, tearful and mournful about it all. He hurried out of the room. He had to suppress his tears. Quickly, Charlie went upstairs to his bedroom so he could deeply mourn for Dorothy.

Charlie was in a state; deeply mournful, bereaved and sad. He stayed in his room until midnight, when he finally decided to come back downstairs.

Meanwhile, Geraldine had stayed in a room downstairs to deeply reflect on Dorothy even more. Geraldine deeply understood things much better and more clearly. As a result of her sorrow and bereavement, she sat with a lacy black veil covering her face. She was a mourner in mourning, dressed in black.

32

Another Talk (Another Ancestral Revelation of Dorothy, an Ancestor)

After Steadman, Mills, Miles, and Kath had popped in to see Geraldine and her parents, they left straightaway. Geraldine went out into the English country garden to rejoin her brother and her mother. Geraldine, Charlie and her mother had a nice tea out in the garden. A garden tea on the terrace.

Geraldine's mother stood up and poured the tea from the teapot into china cups sat on saucers. She followed by putting a dash of fresh milk and spoons of granulated sugar into each cup, and stirring. They all drank a nice cupful of tea, enjoying the refreshing taste. This stimulant - the caffeine - kept a lethargic and sleepy Geraldine awake and alert. Geraldine was sweating and dehydrated in the sweltering sun. Her black camisole top was sweat-soaked from her perspiration.

"Now, dear, have you found out anything about Dorothy?" said Geraldine's mother as she sipped her tea.

"Yes, have you?" asked her brother.

Geraldine was deeply thoughtful as she responded in a mournful way with a sorrowful response.

"Yes. I have. I found out about Dorothy's character when she was a teenager. She was a tomboy. She was tough, rough, resilient and moralistic. That all changed when she attended a convent. She of course wasn't really a true catholic, so how she was allowed to go there is beyond me. Dorothy left the convent, and really missed it. It turned her world upside down, it really did! Dorothy now had to face the realities of life. Her new, adoptive parents looked after her and cared for her. Dorothy was a pampered orphan. She had a natural flair for fashion, and beautiful dress sense. Dorothy had such style and finesse. She loved fashion and new shoes. That sort of thing. All types of footwear. She also liked to read romances - all of that girlie stuff! Dorothy took advantage of her wild romances! But none of it really worked out. It just didn't happen at all. Dorothy was chatty. At home and away, all she did was talk to her friends - gossip even. At her own house and in their homes, Dorothy would say her catchphrase: *'I am going to be someone. What, I just don't know!'* Ultimately she *did* become someone - an elite! - it's remarkable! Dorothy, a peasant, ended up being married to a cobbler. A VIP, truly, in his own right.

Dorothy was obsessed with footwear. It was an obsession! This shoe-lover had far more perfect shoes, slippers and boots than anyone else in the land. Dorothy's shoes had to look new and perfect. If they had a speck of dirt or anything else that left a tarnish on the material, she would change them. She was fussy. That was her. Dorothy was so obsessional."

All of sudden, Charlie interrupted his sister speaking. He looked down at his own shoes; black, leather lace-ups.

"Mine aren't new, are they?" he asked.

Their distracted mother glanced down at her own shoes too, "Nor are mine," she smiled.

Geraldine moved from her seated position and looked at her newish pair of shoes, which were in good condition, "Mine are new," she said proudly.

Sweltering in the hot sun, Geraldine rose from the chair on the terrace. She smartened up and preened herself as she stood, running her fingers through her long, thick, shiny hair. Geraldine was dehydrated from sitting and facing the sun. the dazzling sun rays had blinded her eyes. Sweating in the hot summer weather, she left her mother and brother and walked back into the country house, where she cooled down indoors.

Going upstairs, sluggishly, to her bedroom, she entered and left her door ajar. Geraldine felt dizzy and faint with dehydration and perspiration. Geraldine ran to her luxury bed and threw herself down onto the soft mattress. Geraldine lay on her bed in a comfortable position. She rested by taking a snooze.

Geraldine awoke hours later to find herself all alone at home.

Tonight was a full moon.

33

Geraldine's Afternoon Reflection on Dorothy

During the midafternoon, Charlie came into the sitting room where his preoccupied sister spent time all alone reflecting on her ancestor, Dorothy. Charlie disturbed his sister, making her lose her concentration on her reflection of Dorothy.

"Well, what else have you found out?" he enquired.

Geraldine thought of the question before answering.

"Dorothy was once an orphan. She was miserable and unhappy living in the orphanage. She had romantic ideals and dreams. She was a romantic and a dreamer - a day dreamer too! Dorothy made friends. She liked them and they liked her. Dorothy would talk to her friends for ages. She was a chatterbox. She would get humiliated and frustrated when others did better than her. She didn't think of herself as being bright; rather a dunce instead. Dorothy felt humiliated by individuals who were smarter, cleverer and sexier than her. This caused her frustration and misery.

Dorothy would have fits and tantrums. She would calm down when she went to a chapel to pray and for sanctuary. Dorothy did feel better when she did this. Dorothy, of course, was great with fashion. It was a flair of hers. She had such panache and style. The way she dressed was so much better than everybody else. Dorothy was beautiful, she really was. She was vain too. Dorothy had romances and dates. However, they didn't live up to her expectations. She was unfulfilled.

Dorothy survived with her good friendships at the orphanage. Certainly others got adopted before her, and some after - who worries about being still unadopted. Dorothy's fortune changed when she got adopted out of the blue. She left the orphanage and left her good orphan friends behind.

Dorothy was relieved to get out. Life became even better due to her adoption and new lifestyle. Dorothy was a much happier person. She was free.

Dorothy had vibes and elegance. She was chic, classy and stylish - she dressed so well. This made all the difference to her life. It transformed her. It made her classy and irresistible. On one occasion, Dorothy had her shoes shined, as she thought they needed a polish. That day, Dorothy fell in love with a cobbler. Dorothy and the cobbler eloped and got married. Dorothy's great collection of footwear simply increased. Dorothy was obsessed," said Geraldine.

Suddenly, the doorbell chimed, the sound of it sonorous.

"Look, I must go! My friend is here," said Charlie impatiently. He ran from the sitting room to the front door to answer it, and went out with his friend.

Geraldine found herself all alone at home again. This time she enjoyed the privacy of yet again being alone at home.

34

Geraldine Took More of Dorothy's Heartbreak

Geraldine stayed in her bedroom to avoid her stroppy and angry mother. Geraldine sat in a comfortable armchair, with her legs uncrossed ungracefully. She looked at her notebook. She flicked through the pages of the notebook. She had highlighted the pages in a red felt-tip pen. She took note of Dorothy's heartbreak. How Dorothy ended up becoming deeply heartbroken when most of the children abandoned and deserted her. It is clear why Dorothy felt a heartrending sadness.

Geraldine's mother came into her daughter's bedroom.

"Aren't you coming down? You have been in your bedroom all day," she said.

Geraldine kept her cool and calm, despite her answer, "Mum, I was hoping to get away from you," she said. "You're a pain in the neck!"

Her mother apologies, "I do say, I am sorry. I really am. It's your father. He's too much for me. It's all been too much for me."

“Yes, I do understand, Mum, I know.”

Geraldine’s mother expressed her interest and concern at her daughter finding out about Dorothy’s past history.

“Anything else you have found out about Dorothy?” she enquired.

“From my findings I have taken more of Dorothy’s heartache. You see, she was heartbroken since the day all the children left her. Living alone as a result of separating from her husband, her drinking problem, her miscarriage, being abandoned by the children and deserted by friends, and the divorce proceedings all led to Dorothy taking her own life.”

Geraldine’s mother took the notebook from her daughter’s hand, “It’s late now. Go to bed,” she demanded.

Geraldine obeyed her mother. She got into bed, her mother tucked her restless and sleep daughter in. She kissed her on the forehead, then said goodnight. She switched the light off before leaving, leaving Geraldine’s bedroom pitch dark, apart from the moonlight casting shadows and moonlit reflections.

35

Four Guests Come to Geraldine's Home

Steadman, Kath, Miles and Mills all came to Geraldine's house. They had all been invited for a drink out in the garden. This summer was fine and glorious. The afternoon had glorious sunny weather, and it was scorching. A scorcher!

Geraldine, Steadman, Miles, Mills and Kath all stayed together as a group out in the garden. A garden table awaited them, already set with crystal glasses of appetisers. They each took a glass of effervescent appetiser. They were all thirsty, and quenched that thirst by drinking it up. They all felt refreshed after their drinks. They each put their empty glass back on the tray on the garden table. It was covered in spilt drink and froth from the frothy appetisers.

"Isn't it great that we are all together?" said Kath happily.

Yes. It's wonderful, what a glorious day. We couldn't have picked a better day, could we?" said Geraldine cheerfully.

Being together was exhilarating, and they felt exuberant and composed. They spent a while standing around talking in a group in the big garden.

"It's a pleasure for us to be here, it really is," said Steadman appreciatively.

Geraldine expressed her joy at them being there at her home, "It's a real pleasure to have you all here with me," she said joyously.

"What would Dorothy think, if she could see us now?" wondered Kath.

"I don't dare to think," said Geraldine.

"Nor us," agreed her friends.

"I wish Dorothy was with us now," said Geraldine dreamily.

Walking together in a group, their shadows emerged, appeared, and then vanished out of sight in the sweltering heat. They all stood out of the dazzling, blazing, shining sun. They were all dehydrated and sweating. All of them felt lethargic, sluggish and faint. They moved somewhere else, away from the hot sun. They stood in the shade. A shady spot.

They all admired and marvelled at the incredible beauty of the fine and lovely garden. Part of the garden was an English country rose garden, with floribunda and primroses on a thick, wooden-framed trellis. All of them felt happy today, from their romantic mood and from feeling excitable. They all wore their best clothes (both of the girls wore their best sundresses). Geraldine and Kath wore slinky sundresses with their tanned back exposed, revealing that they were attractive and curvaceous. They wore black slippers. Miles and Mills wore their best Sunday clothes. They obviously all knew they would have to do so, realising that at any time now, they could be intruded upon by Geraldine's intrusive family invading their privacy.

They walked in a group back to the house, and went into a large room filled with antiques and furniture. Geraldine, Miles, Kath and Mills all stood together by the far wall on the opposite side. They glanced at the portraiture, and then looked at the portrait of Dorothy. They all admired and marvelled at the portrait. They all stood looking at it for a long time without realising it. They were unaware and oblivious of their existence. Did time stand still? Did the clocks go back? The grandfather clock chimed. Geraldine grieved for Dorothy.

"We shan't forget you Dorothy," said Geraldine mournfully.

Kath, standing next to Geraldine, whispered in her ear in a childish, childlike fashion, "We promise that we shan't either!"

36

A Winter Warmth and Goodwill

On a cold midwinter's day, Geraldine stayed in the reception room of her home for a short time. She spent time standing there in the middle of the room. Geraldine moved about gracefully, forwards, backwards, and sideways, reflecting on her ancestor, Dorothy. In a dreamy state, Geraldine looked out of the window. Geraldine appeared to be daydreaming. Geraldine was calm and relaxed. She was in deep contemplation, engaged in introspection and retrospection. At once, Geraldine left the reception room. Geraldine came into a large room with lovely antiques and furniture, including a suite and fine decor. She warmed up in the warmer room. She waited in the room for a few guests to arrive. She anticipated her best friends coming.

When they arrived at her parent's house, the housekeeper brought Geraldine's friends into the room.

"Help yourselves to tea, all of you," said Geraldine.

Mills, Miles and steadman each took a teacup and saucer from the silver tray on the table. They all sat down in a group. They all warmed up from the fire in the fireplace, keeping themselves warm in the heat. They all drank their tea.

"You're a lady aren't you, how are you coping?" asked Miles.

"I try to, I really do. I try to be down to earth, isn't that the best way?" smiled Geraldine.

Miles referred to the situation of Geraldine's lifestyle, "That's the point. You can't live like that, how everybody else lives," he pointed out.

Geraldine thought of her culture and cultural lifestyle.

"My parents are wealthy. I do live the highlife. Is it glamorous? That's a matter of opinion. I do try to be ordinary and fit in."

"We do too," said her friends.

Geraldine realised full well that the class system in this country is simply the same strata in general society. Geraldine stirred her tea with a silver teaspoon.

"We do live in a class system. That we do. Do I like it? Well, I am born into it. I do have a silver spoon in my mouth," said Geraldine unashamedly.

Miles actually thought of the British class system in society, "It has always been like that," he said. "Is it likely to change?"

"Yes, will it change?" wondered Mills.

Miles questioned the key factors, "What are the implications? Will it die out? Will there be an influx of people from all backgrounds taking over?"

Geraldine deliberated on that. He was showing his ignorance. She didn't want to answer the question.

"I dare say, I don't know the answer to that," she said.

Steadman observed Geraldine's typical and usual aristocratic ways, "You are not going out as much these days, are you?" he commented.

Geraldine shrugged her shoulders.

"I don't think I am. Not as much as I was. Nope. It's not easy. Things are hard. These days I am far more withdrawn. It's only today that I have invited you round. I Don't wish to be with an earl. I don't wish to be a countess either. At times like these I don't consider myself as one," said Geraldine sullenly.

"Yes, you are extroverted," said Miles.

"Not me, not this time. Maybe today. I'll probably go back to being an introvert. That's more like me," replied Geraldine.

"Are you afraid?" asked Miles.

Geraldine answered, her response honest, "Me? No. Not me! I try not to be."

Mills admired Geraldine, especially her resilience and buoyancy.

"Yes, you cope well, " he remarked.

Geraldine admitted to her ways, "I try to. My religion helps me. I am religious, you just have to be in this day and age. There is just no way around it."

"It sure does help," said Miles.

"I'm not religious," admitted Steadman, "I would say I'm more political than anything else. But that doesn't mean I think of it as claptrap."

Geraldine thought of Steadman as being upper class and for being outspoken. A decent gentleman.

Geraldine expressed her pathos, empathy and ethics, "These days things do get out of hand. Out of control," she said.

"That's why we need to take measures," gestured Miles.

"Quite," agreed Steadman.

Geraldine, an aristocrat, thought of the aristocracies and said, "It is not normal, being an aristocrat. It is not, is it?!"

"No, it certainly is not!" Steadman affirmed.

They all rose from their seats and came out of the room and into another room. The room was much larger with far more paintings and portraits in it. They all went towards the opposite wall, and stood to face it. They all looked at the portraiture on the walls everywhere. Catching glimpses of portraits, then all paying attention to one portrait in particular. An ancestor and descendant.

They all stood still together in a group for a long time, admiring and marvelling at the portrait of Dorothy. Her spirit felt alive. They must have all been completely oblivious of the time they spent looking at the portrait of Dorothy. They must have stood there for at least an hour with their awe, reverie, fondness, love and great admiration for Dorothy.

PART TWO

1

Gingerbread Men

Teri came home from grammar school. Entering the kitchen she joined her mother and Geraldine (who had come to visit), and her younger brother, Robert. Robert was eating a mouthful of peanuts that he gobbled from his hand.

Geraldine watched Teri, a beautifully uniformed schoolgirl, take a biscuit tin from a plastic carrier bag. She opened the rusty biscuit tin lids and showed them all her chocolate-coated gingerbread men. Robert peered at them admiringly,

"You made those? They're good! Can I have some?" he asked.

"Did you do that?" asked Geraldine.

"Yes, I sure did. Do you like them? Miss did the buttons on them. They are brown gingerbread men, just like me," Teri chuckled.

"They're so decorative, how did you do that?" asked Geraldine.

"It's a glace. Miss helped me. Miss has a knack for it - which is more than I can say for my home economics group," answered Teri.

Robert was moving his hand forwards, reaching towards the opened tin on the kitchen table.

"Hands off!" scowled his sister.

"Why not?"

"Get off! You can have one later," yelled Teri.

"Alright then," blushed Robert.

"Get into your things," demanded their mother.

Teri obeyed her mother and did what she was told. She quickly left the kitchen and went upstairs to her bedroom to change. Meanwhile, Geraldine came into the dining room to set the table. Some of the family sat together at the dining table and ate gingerbread men for pudding. Robert ate a bowlful of gingerbread with thick custard. The others either also had lashings of custard, or simply ate theirs plain.

Mostly everyone ate theirs, but Geraldine only ate some of it. Her appetite was gone due to anxiety and for waiting too long.

Robert liked his rich rum-flavoured gingerbread very much. It was a treat he took for granted. With unappreciation he showed a lack of gratitude for his sister, who took all that time and preparation to make it, with assistance from her home economics teacher to bake it (Teri's teacher also assisted by adding decorative touches like glace and buttons.)

After Geraldine had finished washing the dishes, they were sparkling and crystal clean. Geraldine then rejoined Teri and her brother Robert back in the living room, where it was warmer, and more spacious, luxurious, and more cosy than any other room in the big house in the suburban neighbourhood.

Robert's eyes lit up, "I liked the gingerbread men, did you?" asked Robert cheerfully.

Geraldine praised Teri for her good cooking and baking, "I liked it. Teri is good at cooking. She has a flair for it. Isn't she good!"

"Me and my father can't cook," said Robert ashamedly.

Suddenly, Geraldine's aunt, who had been eavesdropping, came into the living room with her arms folded. She approached them and interrupted,

"My dear, you should learn," she said.

Geraldine repeated herself, "I really did like the gingerbread men your sister made."

"Yeah, you did," said Robert. "Isn't that a story?"

Geraldine emphasised Teri's cooking ability. She possessed the qualities of baking and cooking.

"Teri makes good gingerbread, she really does. She's a better cook than she thinks," said Geraldine emphatically.

Teri cheered up with Geraldine's praise, "I do try, that I do. I like cooking, it's something I'm really good at," she said modestly.

Geraldine encouraged Teri to cook and bake and learn to utilise her utility skills in cooking. Sometimes

Teri would invite her friends for dinner by cooking for them at her home. Occasionally, Teri would also cook for them at their homes. Teri took pleasure in cooking. For Teri, cooking was a good interest of hers. Her passion for cooking had developed since womanhood.

Geraldine's mother came round to her sister's. Both Geraldine and her mother brought up the topic of cooking. Both mother and daughter have an interest in cooking respectively. Geraldine's mother was quite good at cooking herself, and also possessed green fingers as well. Geraldine's aunt was even better at cooking. Her aunt tended to do nice country cooking, and in particular homemade dishes which were a country speciality. Geraldine also loved Italian, Greek and Mediterranean dishes - far more than typical, traditional English food (she liked exotic Chinese and oriental food too.) These savoury dishes were really tasty!

At another time, Geraldine and her mother spent time together in a downstairs reception room. They both shared a common interest for cooking and food. They ended up having a good conversation about food and drink, as well as cooking. Geraldine saw an open cookery book with glossy, beautiful pictures. Geraldine wishes to buy new cookery books herself. Her mother and her aunt have a good collection of cookery books themselves. They had collected a lot of volumes.

2

Geraldine's Change of Heart (Geraldine's Love Deepens for the Grandchildren)

At the weekend, all of the grandchildren came over to Geraldine's parents' home. Actually, Geraldine enjoyed being with the grandchildren - granddaughters and a grandson. Geraldine preferred it more than anything else. With the sweet granddaughters she played with their dolls, and with the pampered grandson she spent time playing soldiers (his obsessive love for toy soldiers was an obsession. An obsession in a child's way.)

The way they played evoked memories of Geraldine's past. Geraldine remembers it all - particularly her childhood. Geraldine found it to be a sweet and pleasurable experience being together with the grandchildren. Nothing else could quite compare. Geraldine's personal love for all of the grandchildren made her feel good. It was the best feeling!

Ultimately the sweetest joy of all is a great love for children, in this case, a group of grandchildren coming to have tea together. They all had rum ice cream and peaches, and cheddar and cucumber sandwiches. This seasonal treat was a rather nice and pleasant one. As a helper, Geraldine tended to them attentively, as the hungry grandchildren sat together at the garden table.

Today was much more of a sweeter treat than last time. On this occasion all of them are on their best behaviour. They are well-behaved and good. They enjoy their time being here with their family. For Geraldine there is no better thing to do than spend time with all of the grandchildren again.

For Geraldine, in comparison, nothing else actually seems to matter anymore. Her deep love for all of the grandchildren remains such a good and great love. For them a much deeper love! Whoever could fathom this deep, natural essence of love!

The love itself was unexplainable and an indescribable emotion. For Geraldine it was a strong, personal love.

Early tomorrow morning, all of the grandchildren would leave to go home (the next day they were departing for an island.) Geraldine just wanted to be with them all again. She just did. She had a wishful desire to spend more time with all of them again. Geraldine has a great love and such a fondness for them, naturally. She desired to be with them all again. It's yet another wish of hers.

3

A Brief Introduction of an Aristocrat

Geraldine both likes and dislikes being an aristocrat. For her, personally, there are advantages and disadvantages of being a member and a part of the aristocracy. Naturally, Geraldine, an aristocrat, did enjoy her privileges.

For Geraldine, the best part of being an aristocrat was the glamorous highlife and glamour. Depending on the situation. For certain members of the aristocracy, their aristocratic lifestyle can be glamorous, tragic, risky, dangerous, and pleasurable.

Geraldine likes travelling, jet setting, and sightseeing. As a sightseer and tourist, she would spend time sightseeing.

Geraldine took pleasure from her privileges by going to estates, palaces, grand houses, mansions, penthouses, villas, and the continent. As usual, Geraldine took it for granted. In some circumstances she was thoughtless, uncaring and ungrateful, expecting too much for being an aristocrat and from the aristocracy.

A typical aristocrat, she was demanding. Making demands, expecting high class travel and service to be provided all of the time. This included luxury accommodation in five-star hotels.

As jet-setters, Geraldine's elitist family had their own private jet, which flew from an international airport. As a private, shy and diffident aristocrat, Geraldine kept away from aristocratic public duties. She left that to other members of the family - in particular, her parents. Subsequently, other members of the family took an active role in charities, charity work, and charity organisations.

4

Geraldine's Need to Fly Away

Geraldine suffered at times with such family worries, burdens and financial difficulties, problems and troubles. Whenever these occurrences happened, Geraldine would take the opportunity to fly away to a romantic location; to an exotic paradise destination. Geraldine had acquaintances who worked for an international airline.

Geraldine had a British passport. She was a British citizen. Naturally, she was patriotic about the United Kingdom. Her own country. Her nation. At times, Geraldine had been disappointed at its failures. It's disappointing. However, this nation was transcendent in any other field. Going on vacation to a romantic and beautiful paradisiacal location made all the difference to Geraldine. A getaway! Geraldine succumbed to and overcame her troubles, and survived her family difficulties, troubles and problems - which unfortunately she had been burdened by.

It's an unfortunate misfortune. With such freedom, Geraldine escaped to the tropics, to a Caribbean island full of paradisiacal exoticism and tropical charm.

5

Geraldine's Vineyard Experience

Geraldine stayed at a chateau in a valley region of Provence. It was a family-run business. A vinery. For Geraldine, her stay with family friends in Provence had been ideal, relating to wine-tasting and spending time with epicures. Geraldine had a liking for quality wine. Red or white, sweet or dry. She liked French and German wine. Though, as a preference, French wine is her favourite. As a casual wine-taster, Geraldine prefers French wine best. For example, Chardonnay and Bordeaux. Geraldine, during the house of the week, ended up staying at a farmhouse for a few days.

Geraldine enjoyed her break in Provence. In particular, working at the vineyard. An environment of thich grape vines everywhere in the vast vineyard. The fresh crops of dry, ripe bunches of green grapes were sweet and juicy. Geraldine was a keen worker, helping them to pick bunches of fresh grapes from the vines. Geraldine spent hours picking grapes with them, and putting them neatly into a wicker basket.

The other families and helpers who were working, gathered the baskets and crates ready for the pressing to be done. All the crops of fresh grapes would be pressed. At the vinery, the wine underwent a process of being pressed and bottled at source.

Geraldine did like her nice experience working at the vineyard as a helper. She felt pleased, overwhelmed, and greatly privileged at being able to pick grapes in a vineyard in the region of Provence. Geraldine looked forward to grape picking again next summer in Provence, with families from the Provencal.

There was another break with the French family from Provence (they were, of course, family friends), and Geraldine stayed for a few days with them at a chateau. She enjoyed this short break away. The French family treated Geraldine to fine vintage wines, a selection of cheese and crackers, and crusty French bread. Geraldine enjoyed this treat. Geraldine drank glasses of vintage wine. The wine was sweet, dry, and fruity.

For Geraldine, the trip met her high expectations. It was a satisfying and overwhelming experience for her - and a romantic one. Geraldine and the French family dined at a lovely restaurant in the square in part of historic and stately Provence.

6

Geraldine's Personal Love of France

Geraldine loved France, especially the French culture, the arts, and the capital city for its fashion (Geraldine was a fashion designer by occupation.) Best of all, Geraldine loved French cuisine, and in particular the champagne and wines. She also preferred the toiletries, perfumes and cosmetics available.

Geraldine also loved her French family friends from Provence. Generally, as a foreigner, she grovelled about France in general. She was ambivalent about models, as she herself was not only attractive, but had a curvaceous figure herself.

Going to Provence was a nice experience; a good one. Geraldine stayed at her French family friends' homes. In the region, Geraldine visited an art gallery, a museum, and dined at a fashionable French restaurant. Another time, she went to a nice typical French cafe in the town square. As a tourist, she took the opportunity to go sightseeing at historical attractions. As a sightseer, she admired the Renaissance landmarks, architecture, and historical sights.

Geraldine also visited the tourist information centre. Tourism was popular in the region, especially during high season. During her stay, Geraldine stayed at a chateau, a farmhouse, and also a townhouse. Geraldine confided in her French family friends, Madame, Monsieur, and Mademoiselle. Geraldine enjoyed her rather great experience. She took the opportunity to brush up on her French, not that she encountered much difficulty with the French language - she was fluent in French, with an affectatious accent that made her sound like a French-born citizen. She spoke with the affectation of a passionate French woman.

Geraldine enjoyed her freedom, liking her peace, quiet, and solitude too. Geraldine indulged in a luxurious sauna and spy. She engaged in escapism and exoticism. Her exciting pleasurable and narcissistic fantasies and dreams filled her with ecstasy and pleasure.

Finally, her short break in provence ended, and Geraldine took a short-haul flight back to England.

7

A Seasonal Break

Before the Christmas season, Geraldine and her parents spent a few days on a nice seasonal break at a log chalet in the Swiss Alps.

Indoors, Geraldine was warm, comfortable, and snug inside the cosy chalet. It was far away from literally everywhere else. This thick, snowy land and picturesque Christmas scenery had alpine and berried trees everywhere, all thickly covered in snow.

Geraldine was enchanted at the Swiss charm. She marvelled at and admired it. It was such a joyful delight. Geraldine daydreamed and romanticised. She was literally lost in her deep ecstasies. Geraldine really did like it immensely in the enchanting Alps; this mountainous region.

Geraldine was cool, calm, joyful, relaxed, happy, exuberant and cheerful. She felt invigorated breathing in the draughty Swiss air. Her warm breath rose in the air. Geraldine felt cooler, calmer, and happier than normal due to having this seasonal break in the Swiss Alps, and because Christmastime was drawing near.

At times, Geraldine avoided her parents because she wanted to be alone. How she does like her own privacy, quietude and solitude! For Geraldine, this Christmas season excited her. It was so exciting. Unfortunately, on this occasion, Geraldine would miss Christmas for certain.

Standing and looking out of a window, she saw a group of children building a snowman. Admiring the sight of it, Geraldine was filled with a childish joy and excitement. Standing still, she watched all of the children play on their sledges and ski. Geraldine was unenthusiastic about skiing. It was something she had no wish, use or desire to do. She would rather spend time designing a new pattern for a dress. Her obsession to design things was quite obsessive. It was an obsessional compulsion of hers.

Geraldine's latest design was something rather good. She would persevere with it at its most early design stages of course. Geraldine must have been oblivious of the time. She must have spent hours designing the latest pattern for a new dress. And this new design was beautiful!

At other times, on other days, Geraldine and her parents dined out at fancy restaurants. At other times they went out into the black forest. It was a strange experience and encounter, although a deeply fascinating place - it's something else! It had a magical charm and beauty, and a natural loveliness that stunned them. Were they under a spell? Any of them? No spell affected them though, as they had their own personal faith and were religious themselves.

In a few days the break was cut short; it hadn't lasted long, but it would shortly be Christmas. Despite that, for Geraldine and her family it was another memorable seasonal break.

During the course of their seasonal time (it was not quite Christmas yet!) Geraldine made a dream dress-design. Her romantic seasonal nights were unforgettable, just before Christmas time.

8

An Excursion

Geraldine and her parents, on another of their days of travel and excursions, stopped off in Malaga, Spain. A popular tourist hotspot, and a lively destination. A vacation resort. Today's hot, sunny weather was sweltering. A scorching Mediterranean heat. This Mediterranean weather was getting hotter and hotter.

Geraldine and her parents sat together outside a cafe. The family sat at a table at the far back. Amongst the holidaymakers and tourists there were lager lout Britons. They were away-supporters, fans staying at the hotels in anticipation of the international football match tomorrow. These thuggish fans had already got their tickets. Geraldine and her parents were tourists and foreigners who did not appear to be embarrassed, annoyed, irritated or irritable.

The British louts - binge drinkers - were possible hooligans. Geraldine and her family thought of these unruly and boisterous groups as thugs and possible hooligans, singing in their slurred, out-of-tune voices, and being a disgrace to their country. These Britons were disgraceful fans who had been appalling.

Geraldine's family tensed up as they sat together at the table. The family had been diffident, anxious and nervous when seated at the table. The threesome drank their drinks in a rush. They left the cafe in a hurry. None of them wanted to come back to this tourist hotspot in Mallorca ever again. They had lost their interest in this holiday resort in particular.

Geraldine and her tired parents walked quite a distance. Reaching the bus stop, they stood and waited, until eventually their bus came. Geraldine and her parents departed. On board the bus they took an excursion back to their luxury hotel. A destination of theirs.

9

Geraldine's Price of Being an Aristocrat

From her home, Geraldine has been driven to a manor house. It was quite a long journey. Finally reaching the grounds of the grand manor house, Geraldine got out of the car. She closed the car door and stood in a position at an angle. Geraldine waved goodbye to her chauffeur before the driver departed. Her chauffeur drove off. Geraldine expected her chauffeur to return tomorrow morning to pick her up and drive her home. After the chauffeur had gone, the automatic electric blue gates had closed.

Waiting at the door was Mr and Mrs Shires. They were expecting and anticipating Geraldine to arrive. They all went upstairs to the top upper room, a suite. Mr and Mrs Shires and Geraldine sat together in the comfort and luxury of the suite. Geraldine warmed up from the nice warmth from the central heating. She rubbed her hands together while looking at a picture that said 'Home Sweet Home' on the decorated wall opposite.

A short time later, a uniformed housemaid wearing an apron, brought them their tea. The housemaid attended to them and served the three of them fresh tea. Mr and Mrs Shires, and Geraldine, each took a china teacup and a saucer. They each drank a teacupful and nibbled plain biscuits.

"Did you get here alright?" asked Mrs Shires

Geraldine luxuriated in a position on a leather armchair (she had a desire to overindulge in luxuries!) She enjoyed the pleasure of comfort with wonder and joy. Geraldine felt cool, calm, serene, placid and peaceful. A lady who appeared to be solicitous in her lady-like way. Geraldine showed a solicitude, which was nice of her. Geraldine was good and well-behaved, especially her demeanour.

"How are you? I have missed you, really I have. Oh! I am so glad to be with you two again. I have missed you both. I do hope everything is alright. All that worrying, it's not good, is it?" said Geraldine concernedly.

Mrs Shires hushed her husband and said, "We are fine, aren't we? Just about coping." She smiled.

Geraldine was relieved that Mr and Mrs Shires had resolved their matters and dealt with their problems.

"Oh good! I am pleased everything is alright now. It's turned out alright in the end. I have been worrying," said Geraldine.

"Did you get here alright?" repeated Mrs Shires.

Geraldine felt restless staying seated on the armchair. She rose and walked over to Mrs Shires, who was sitting on a settee next to her husband. Standing, Geraldine touched Mrs Shires' shoulder. A light touch.

"I got here alright," she answered.

"Did you do anything nice?" asked Mrs Shires.

Geraldine acknowledged Mrs Shires, and appreciated the concern for her, "Yes, I did," she said. "I forgot about the time I worked on a dress pattern. A new design of mine. Hopefully it will turn out well."

Mrs Shires leaned forward in her seat. Clasping both her hands together, Mrs Shires (a dame), glanced up.

"Good! that's what I like to hear," she said.

"How's life?" asked Mr Shires.

Initially, Geraldine thought of aristocracy and how aristocrats were: full of avarice, materialistic, wordly-wise, elistits, cosmopolitan, landowners and tycoons, with their trusts, estates and legacies. She hesitated to answer.

"Life to me is just the same as always. No different at all! I suppose the only sort of difference at this time is that I do now have more time on my hands. In the past I just didn't have any time for myself to do anything that I wanted," said Geraldine honestly.

Mr Shires was bleary-eyed, and adjusted his eyesight and vision by wearing a pair of glasses.

"Oh I can see! Tell me, how are you finding life now?" enquired Mr Shires.

Geraldine admitted, "It's great, it really is! I am not that keen on being an aristocrat. I do prefer to be quite ordinary, and for my life to be simple. I do not wish to be an aristocrat, or even thought of as a countess at all. It is daunting for me! It's just not for me. There are good things and bad things about it. These days I just want to be free. Nothing else. I just hope to continue being free! I don't want anything else," murmured Geraldine.

Mrs Shires put her hand on Geraldine's. Mr Shires touched Geraldine. She felt his soft touch - an affectionate one.

"We do have hope for you," said Mrs Shires self-assuredly.

Geraldine felt hopeful, positive, and optimistic about her future, "Well I'm glad someone does," she said sardonically. She paused and added, "I dislike being an aristocrat. I don't like it. Not at all! All this intrusion, and not having any privacy."

"Be positive," said Mrs Shires. "There must be good things about it."

"All the glamour and highlife just is not for me. Concerning aristocracy - what is it exactly? How do you actually define it? It's a status, yes. A class for the privileged. It is. It's elitist. A jet set. At times I really dislike it, and at other times, I love it. You do get the best of everything. You have a personal jet, best hotels, villas, fashion, brands. Is it glamour? Is it glamorous? It could well be. But at times it is the total opposite. The public and people do tend to get the wrong impression. On the contrary, it is risky and dangerous, and at times, evil. The highlife - do I like it? Well, do I? I've kind of gotten used to it over the decades. At times, I do prefer to be like some kind of hermit or recluse. Life has made me feel this way. Perhaps to be in a sanctuary of my own would be the best thing," blurted out Geraldine.

Geraldine blinked from the bright lights. She felt rather sleepy. She got up from the nice comfortable armchair. Geraldine was feeling lethargic and exhausted, so she left them. She went upstairs to a spare bedroom, where she stayed overnight. Feeling sleepy, she lay down on the luxurious bed. She luxuriated in a comfortable position on the mattress, and within minutes she had dozed off. Geraldine slept like a child.

10

Geraldine Declares Her Decline at Making Appearances at Venues

Geraldine declined to do any public engagements or functions because she tended to be paranoid and fearful, as well as feeling vulnerable and exposed. Geraldine tried to cope with her personal problems, ordeals and traumas, but she struggled to overcome them. Geraldine just didn't want to take on any unnecessary responsibilities or commitments. Besides, she appeared to be unfit and unsuitable to take on the role at walkabouts, venues, institutes, and institutions. Furthermore, Geraldine was shy and timid when assigned for public engagements, walkabouts and functions.

Geraldine left all of that to certain individuals within the family - ones who were suitable and fit for it! Those certain ones had a good demeanour and reputation. Although Geraldine did not engage in public engagements and functions, she did in fact offer her services for free. With an obligation, an obligatory willingness, to offer and provide assistance at certain functional times at engagements. Personally, Geraldine dismissed any such claims of neglect and negligence!

11

Embankment

On another cold day, Geraldine felt traumatised yet again, suffering from trauma. At the time, this calm, cook and adrenalised passenger did actually seem to be coping quite well, despite the family ordeal she had experienced.

Geraldine was on the underground, heading towards the line she needed. As she approached the 'WAY OUT' and went up the stairs, she met a good friend who was waiting for her. Geraldine depended on her female friend, a beautiful and voluptuous city secretary; a redhead.

From the embankment, Geraldine and her streetwise friend saw a homeless man on the street. The man was known as 'Junkman.' Both his wife and only daughter had deserted him. He had been abandoned. Geraldine kept calm and cool. Geraldine showed her concern, but was unable to help his situation. She was aware of this homeless man's case. She knew him by sight. Geraldine looked at this homeless man with such deep sympathy and compassion.

This sympathiser has an urge and incentive to do something. She had a purposeful initiative that she was inclined to have fulfilled. Geraldine ended up using her standing and power, and that of her relative, to get this cold, homeless man off the streets. Subsequently, both aristocrats negotiated with the proper authorities, and the homeless man was housed, fed and taken care of.

Geraldine did a good deed, she felt solace at having done it.

12

Nightmare

Yesterday night, Geraldine had a nightmare. She stayed in her bedroom from the morning until mid-afternoon. She still felt enervated, tired, lethargic and moody. During the course of the day, Geraldine rested for a long time in her bedroom. When she had recovered, she felt much better.

Hours later, Geraldine came downstairs to go into the lounge alone. Suddenly, her father came in through the back door, having been gardening during the late Sunday afternoon. It was a nice day. The weather was hot and sunny.

With concern, Geraldine's father wondered what was wrong with his daughter. Standing, he looked at her with such love,

"Why aren't you dressed?" he asked.

Geraldine, in a sulk, admitted to her father, "I couldn't sleep. I had a nightmare."

"Well! What!" said her father impatiently.

Geraldine didn't answer. Her father prompted her again, pressing for an answer. Geraldine was still wearing her slinky, figure-hugging black nightdress, and a black dressing gown, which was left untied and loose.

Geraldine stood by her father. She folded her arms while swaying her hips gracefully.

"You see, I couldn't sleep. Not a wink. I had a nightmare. A bad one. It was awful. When was it? I just can't remember. It was terrible in the least," she shuddered.

"Love! Stay in and rest," said her father sympathetically.

Geraldine thought of it. Geraldine has been fearful, she feared for her life! She shrugged and nodded,

"I really should, shouldn't I?"

"Geraldine, you must get spiritual. Wise up. Go to church. Read the word. You must! Weren't you once a Sunday school girl?!" insisted her father.

"Oh! I was. That I was for sure!" smiled Geraldine.

Her father was worried about her, "Do be careful and wary of who you mix with. Don't talk to just anyone. Be vigilant. Be private. I insist! Keep things private and confidential," he advised.

Listening, an attentive Geraldine paid heed to her father. She, of course, realised that her father was intent on warning her.

"Oh, yes! I will certainly take note of your sound advice," responded Geraldine.

The concerned father agitated his daughter again. This time he warned her by instructing and advising her,

"You're naive, you really are. How many times have I told you? Are you listening to me? You must wise up. Don't let individuals take advantage of you. You must not be gullible. Don't make yourself vulnerable. Where on earth is your common sense? Don't worry! Don't be hasty and frantic - which is what you are. Do read the word. Believe," he urged.

"Yes! I will. I shall do that," assured Geraldine.

"Are you afraid?" asked her father.

"Well, no," Geraldine paused. "Not now. I feel alright, really. I do. I feel alright with you."

Her father paid heed to his daughter, and took notice of how his daughter stuttered (Geraldine tended to stammer whenever she was nervous, anxious, or afraid.) With wisdom, Geraldine's father spoke up,

"You really must try and get used to it. You must not be naive! You must experience it for yourself. Do get experienced," he warned.

"Yes, I must," Geraldine agreed. She obeyed her father by doing as she was told. She was obedient to her father. Her father was tolerant.

At once, Geraldine left her father. Shivering in the cold house, everywhere cool and shady in shadows and reflections. Geraldine slowly went back upstairs, back to her cool bedroom. Geraldine, keeping her cool, felt sluggish and calm. She slumped in an armchair near the corner of the wall. She spent time reading the word.

Reading the word daily was something habitual and obsessive that Geraldine did every day.

Geraldine engaged in meditation, mortification and discipline. On the disciplinary basis of her faith (including reading, praying and worshipping.) Afterwards, Geraldine worshipped. A worshipper! This believer felt alive, well, better, and healthy too.

13

Geraldine's Dislikes

Geraldine's mother stayed at home. She stayed with her calm daughter in the lounge. At that present time, Geraldine took the opportunity to confide in her mother. Her mother was displeased with her lazy and idle daughter.

"Aren't you going to work today?" she questioned.

"No! Not me! I am staying in. I am too tired and overworked," groaned Geraldine.

"Well don't make it a habit. Do your work. Get it done! You're slacking," grumbled her mother.

Geraldine kept calm while sitting next to her mother on a settee. She was enjoying her quietude and freedom. A day off from work made all the difference to Geraldine's health. Since Geraldine's adolescence, these ethics and attitudes had constantly drummed at her mind. This application of doing work was an obsession.

"Why on earth do we do all this work? One *should* work, yes, we must, but one should set a good balance between work, rest and leisure," expostulated Geraldine.

"I quite agree. In your case. You must be disciplined at your work. Discipline is crucial. It is the key to succeed in work. I have stressed this to you lots of times. So do take heed," said her mother matter-of-factly.

"Mum, I do understand that. But it's besides the point. One does have to set a complete balance between work, rest and leisure. That's a pleasure. That's the point I am really trying to make," objected Geraldine.

"Yes, love! Well said! I quite agree," smiled her mother.

At present, Geraldine enjoyed the comfort of being pleasurably comfortable from luxuriating in such pleasurable luxury from her position. A luxurious lounge with a fine suite of sumptuous quality. Geraldine concluded her displeasure, fears, phobias and anxieties that she faced daily as a result of being the daughter of an aristocratic family.

"I dislike being an aristocrat. If that's what I am, I'm tired and fed up with it! I dislike this aristocratic lifestyle. I really do. Yes, there are times at which I do like it, of course. I do not like being undesirable. I do hate all of this hatred, oppression, intimidation, danger and crime that goes on in society and in the world," grumbled Geraldine.

Listening, her mother confirmed her acknowledgement of her daughter's phobias.

"Look, I do understand what you are saying. There is no going back. This is the life we live. There is nothing in hell that's going to change it. So let's not forget the issue. It has to be dealt with. I'm afraid you have to cope with it. It's our life. Our lifestyle. Our lives are of the aristocracy, so get on with it, live it! There's nothing we can do about it. We can hide and run away, but for how long? We can avoid it, dress it down and play it down. But we can't keep running away and hiding, we have to face it," said Geraldine's mother sternly.

Geraldine listened, and agreed with what her passionate mother had said, "Yes! Face up to it!"

"Time to face the music," concluded her mother.

14

The Definition

Geraldine's personal tailor arrived at her home. The tailor was punctual on his arrival. Geraldine was expecting her tailor at that time, and she answered the front door and welcomed him in. They both went upstairs to a bedroom with a mirrored wardrobe and a dressing table. The professional and exclusive tailor took Geraldine's body measurements by using a tape measure he had brought with him.

Geraldine stood still. The tailor expertly calculated her measurements. He double-checked again to make certain he'd taken the right measurements. The expert tailor admired Geraldine's admirable figure. Geraldine was attractive. She was indeed looking lovely wearing a slinky black dress, glossy tights, and low-heeled slippers.

"Is it alright? How is it?" asked Geraldine.

"Nothing's changed. Not to worry, the measurements are about the same," replied the tailor.

"Do you like working with the upper class?" asked Geraldine.

"Oh yes! Why shouldn't I? Of course! They are my clients and customers," smiled the tailor.

Geraldine admitted her discontentment and dissatisfaction, "I am getting tired and fed up of being an aristocrat. I really dislike it at times. What is the point of it all? It's the same 'this,' the same 'that.' It's the same stuck-up people. Frankly, I have had enough of it. Why should I have to put up with it? What is the definition of an aristocrat and the aristocracy? It's a social class. A privileged, elite group in a hugely fashionable society. Their society. I must add and admit, that at times I do wish I was just an ordinary person. Why aren't I? Not having to put up with all this hoo-ha! There is too much stress, trouble, and problems to face, cope and deal with. It's just not for me. My family copes well with it, they really do. They like it, whereas I hate it. At times I just can't stand it! It isn't for me!" grumbled Geraldine.

"Oh, never mind," commiserated the tailor.

Geraldine touched the tailor affectionately, appreciating his thoughtful consideration for her.

"I shall ring you and let you know about the fitting of your garment. Give me until next week, and I shall be in touch," said the tailor.

Geraldine quickly showed the tailor out of the house. Standing in the doorway, Geraldine waved goodbye and watched him drive away in his vintage car. Geraldine was pleased to have seen her tailor, and that he had attended to her and taken her measurements. Geraldine wondered if the tailor would consider making another item for when this one was done. Another dress.

Geraldine was filled with anxiety. In this instance she had totally lost interest in women's fashion and fashion design. Geraldine worried about her problems yet again. A constant worrier who was worrying about her future.

Geraldine came back into the quiet lounge. There was silence. There she stayed for the rest of the day, doing nothing else. Geraldine took her time to rest and relax in comfort. She lay down on a settee. From her position she took comfort from being comfortable. She rounded off the night by reading a romance and then listening to soul music.

During the course of the next week, Geraldine received a glossy gift box with a pretty ribbon. It was delivered by a delivery driver. Geraldine was excited, she untied the ribbon of the pretty, feminine box. She took out a new sequinned dress. The dress the tailor had made.

Geraldine tried on the new dress and looked at herself in the wardrobe mirror. She admired the new dress. Geraldine was narcissistic about her fine figure! Geraldine looked at herself admirably. She favoured her tailor more than ever before! Geraldine preferred her tailor to anyone else. She was so proud! Geraldine made a fleeting appearance as a guest at a ball. She took great pride in wearing her new favourite dress. Those that saw her that night said that she took their breath away. Geraldine was personal and engaging.

15

Geraldine's Stint as a Fashion Model Abroad

An agent representing Geraldine, negotiated a contract with a top modelling agency. Subsequently, Geraldine engaged in modelling by doing photoshoots, and modelling as a fashion model down catwalks in capital cities.

As a fashion model, Geraldine enjoyed her pleasurable experiences. Although she modelled for a considerable time, she ended up giving it up due to her fears and phobias.

A fear of paranoia and being paranoid, Geraldine dreaded becoming undesirable, as she was vain and narcissistic. A typical narcissist, in a way. She took pride in appearing in fashion shows, galas, and doing various photoshoots with highly professional fashion photographers. At times, the temperamental male photographer had been difficult for her to work with. This conceited photographer expected too much, and certain conditions were stipulated. Finally, in the end, Geraldine gave it all up (such a short-lived modelling career; apparently she was forced out by saboteurs within the modelling agency, other models, and photographers.)

Geraldine, a fashion model, experienced sabotage during photoshoots and modelling assignments all over the continent, the Caribbean, and the islands of the Indian Ocean. These beautiful tropical islands were exotic and paradisiacal. A tropical exoticism!

Generally, Geraldine was extroverted - though this would change as she became more withdrawn, eventually becoming introverted and housebound. Did she fear that she was undesirable? Losing her good looks and beauty? Geraldine did actually enjoy her short-lived stint as a fashion model. Consequently, she became bitterly disappointed when it was all over for her. Nevertheless, she relished the fond, memorable experiences of doing modelling assignments all over the world.

Geraldine remained reserved, coy, and reticent. She tended not to talk or share anything about her experiences with any of her family members, or anybody else whatsoever. Geraldine was secretive. It was too personal. She kept it to herself! Regarding her secrets, Geraldine was inclined to never blurt out any of them to outsiders - not even to newcomers who were entering the modelling world for the first time.

16

Geraldine Stays at Her Aunt's

Geraldine stayed at her aunt's at her home. Going to her aunt's residence made such a personal difference to Geraldine; it made her feel much better. Geraldine preferred it at her aunt's residence. It was her preference compared to any other homes she was used to staying in.

Geraldine loved art, she was something of an aesthete and a connoisseur. She also admired architecture, structures, structural foundations and elevations. She had relatives who were architects and surveyors - and one who was an archaeologist. Another relative, from Geraldine's extended family, was a marine. Geraldine liked music too. She had a real interest in it.

As a fashion designer, Geraldine was obsessed with fashion. She had a passion and an obsession for fashion. Her aesthetic taste in fashion changed according to the seasons and the latest trends, and in accordance with her likes and dislikes too of course.

Geraldine's aunt was nice, caring and loving. With affection, she pampered her niece. Geraldine preferred her beloved aunt over everybody else. Geraldine would normally confide in her aunt, talking to her for hours.

Geraldine was being loquacious again (she was often referred to as a chatterbox by her mum, her friends, relatives, colleagues and acquaintances.)

Geraldine regarded her aunt with such fondness. And the aunt loved her niece.

"You're here with me. It's good we are together," smiled Geraldine's aunt. In the refurbished lounge, both aunt and niece sat together on a luxury settee. Relaxing in comfort, "Look, I know how much you hate being an aristocrat, but there really is nothing you can do about it, is there? It's life! You really must get on with it. Do the best that you can do under the circumstances. It isn't easy. Please keep reading God's word. I urge you. You'll never go wrong, I can assure you," promised her aunt.

Geraldine tried to keep calm and cool, "That's fine! Coming from you!" she snapped.

"If in doubt, please come and talk to me," urged her aunt.

Normally the niece would listen to her aunt's advice. Geraldine thought a lot of her aunt as a mellow agony aunt. She was a hugely experienced librarian, and an intellectual who had undertaken her studies and training, ultimately reaching transcendence in her field. Geraldine obeyed her aunt by listening to her advice.

"I'm sure I will. I shall do so," she assured her aunt.

Geraldine's aunt moved position and clasped her hands together, "Good," she smiled.

"I'm tired. I'm going to bed. Goodnight!" said Geraldine.

It was late, and Geraldine felt tired, exhausted and sleepy. She decided to leave her aunt to go upstairs to her bedroom - it was later than her usual bedtime.

Geraldine's aunt hadn't missed her niece. Also, she had seen her a few days ago when she had popped in briefly to see her sister.

The following day, Geraldine felt free. She took joy in her freedom. That day, she spent more time with her aunt.

17

Geraldine's Times of Leisure

Geraldine, at leisure, enjoyed going to a museum, art gallery, theatre and to the park. Going to these public places as an interest of hers. Geraldine took in an art exhibition, looking at artists' and painters' works in various sections of the art gallery. Today's exhibition at the modern art gallery featured a selection of various painters and artists.

Geraldine, a dilettante, hoped to look for a masterpiece! Would she actually see one? Were there any of them at the current exhibition? Geraldine walked ahead of her friend, going from section to section of the grand art gallery. She left her friend lagging behind, reading the details of every artist and painter.

Geraldine, with an obsessive fascination, was self-absorbed and enjoyed the distinctive works of art. The dilettante and her friend spent about an hour looking at the exhibition in the gallery.

Going to the gallery made a nice change, as Geraldine was usually too busy, occupied and obsessed with designing her dress patterns. Geraldine enjoyed her time at the art gallery. Oh how she liked it! The best thing about it for Geraldine was the joy, pleasure and freedom of admiring artists' and painters' works of art.

That was the joyful pleasure of it; admiring the admirable painters and artists, with certain artists having their own collections of their work on display.

After about an hour, Geraldine left the art gallery with her friend. Geraldine had been overwhelmed with such inspirational joy. She took delight and pleasure in admiring these famous painters' and artists' works at the exhibition. The exhibition only lasted until Autumn.

On another occasion, Geraldine went with her family to a museum where they saw prehistoric dinosaur exhibits. The strange thing about Geraldine's visit and admission to the museum, was that she forgot about everything. Did she have amnesia? Was it actually something in the past she had seen at the museum when she was only a mere girl? This could have been a forgotten memory of Geraldine's. Geraldine simply reliving her actual past.

On another occasion, Geraldine and her parents went to a theatre. In the auditorium, the audience watched a 'whodunnit' - a murder mystery. Geraldine, a keen theatre-goer, was overwhelmed by this suspenseful mystery play, because her family had been given a nice treat by a member of Geraldine's extended family. They had treated them to complimentary tickets, courtesy of the theatre.

On another occasion, with her father, Geraldine went to a park. Geraldine liked spending time with her father. They walked around the park, looking at pigeons, ducks, swans and geese on a pond. They looked at the shimmering reflection in the water. In the park they saw mothers pushing the prams of their sons or daughters. Geraldine liked this park. It was one of her favourites. She liked the peace and quiet, and the freedom.

Geraldine felt cool, calm and peaceful. Being with her father made it incredibly special for Geraldine, since she hadn't seen him for days. Walking around the park, Geraldine admired the sights. It was prettier and lovelier than ever in the summertime. The park was naturally beautiful and colourful. For Geraldine, the park was such a joy and a delight. It was even more special during the glorious sunny weather. Today was a much hotter day, and Geraldine cherished the time with her father.

18

Geraldine Spent a Day With the Grandchildren

A parent dropped off their grandson and granddaughter. They arrived at Geraldine's house. Geraldine had been anticipating and expecting their arrival from Kent. Geraldine got great pleasure playing with the grandson and granddaughter. For hours she played with their favourite toys and dolls. Geraldine experienced such bliss, joy, satisfaction and pleasure playing with the grandchildren. The actual joy and emotion Geraldine did feel was a greater feeling than anything else she had ever experienced. It was an even better feeling than the babysitting she had done the day before for someone she knew well.

Geraldine spent the day playing with the playful and excitable grandchildren. The grandson was boisterous, excited and playful, while the granddaughter was well-behaved, quiet, happy, and lackadaisical. There was an animated childish playfulness between them. Geraldine joined in and played with them in spells during the course of the day. Oh how she loved them.

Geraldine got such joy and happiness playing with them both. She felt such sweet bliss and joy being together with them. Geraldine became rejuvenated, regenerated, blissful and joyful spending a long day with the happy grandchildren, who stayed and played for most of the day.

During the midsummer evening, the children's parents, and their driver, arrived punctually by car to pick them up and drive them home. It was only a short journey.

Geraldine looked forward to them both coming to her home again.

19

Geraldine's Setback (Another Disappointment)

Geraldine received bad feedback concerning the fashion collection she had collaborated on with other fashion designers. She was informed by her miserable and disappointed colleague that the collaboration hadn't been successful. Neither of them got the success they hoped for. It was another setback for Geraldine, and very disappointing.

Her mother, Fran, insisted that she tell her about the summer fashion collection she had collaborated on with other female designers. She pressed her daughter for an answer.

"Well, what is it?" she asked crossly.

"It's disappointing for me. It really is. It's disappointing for all of us," Geraldine answered.

Fran scowled, "All that bloody money. What a waste!" she snapped.

Geraldine stayed quite calm in spite of her misery, "Yes. Quite," she blushed.

"Will you ever learn?" sighed her mother unsympathetically.

Geraldine admitted her failure, "I know I have failed," she said. "It's disappointing for us."

"Stop this bloody spending," said her mother angrily.

Geraldine kept silent. She felt humiliated and embarrassed at her failure of course. Geraldine was disappointed and unhappy. She stood still with her arms folded gracefully.

"I will, mother. I will," she sulked.

"You really aren't as good as you make yourself out to be," criticised her mother.

"Oh mum! Don't!" said Geraldine miserably. She stormed out of the room and ran upstairs to her bedroom. She locked herself in, turning the brass key in the lock.

Geraldine ended up staying in her bedroom night and day.

20

Geraldine Likes Her Time Alone

It rained again. A torrential rain. Geraldine stayed in her bedroom. The heavy downpour lasted for hours. Geraldine was in a romantic mood, hearing the raindrops spluttering on the bedroom windows. She felt electrified by the sound of the elements, natural sensations and the electrifying atmosphere. Geraldine took pleasure in the luxurious comfort of her boudoir. She was wrapped in a thick blanket, snug in her cosy boudoir. In this pleasurable comfort, Geraldine luxuriated on a couch and daydreamed. Geraldine daydreamed through the course of the murky, cold, rainy day.

Geraldine liked her peace and quiet, and her freedom, as well as being all alone at home. It made it even more special to have her privacy too. It was a joyful and delightful feeling. An exhilaration. Geraldine took such pleasure in the comfort of being indoors all alone in her luxurious boudoir.

21

Geraldine's Stern Father Scolds Her

Whenever Geraldine had any problems, anxieties, or troubles, she tended to keep herself to herself at home. Geraldine seemed relatively experienced about things in general. She knew how to cope and deal with most circumstances, and her family was experienced and familiar with situations such as libel, scandals and lawsuits. Her family pressed her to conduct herself well, and to be well-behaved.

From time to time, her parents reminded their daughter of her previous bad behaviour and conduct. Both her parents, again and again, reprimanded Geraldine about her misconduct and misbehaviour, and had to remind her again to have good conduct and behaviour. They insisted on it!

Had young Geraldine, an aristocrat, kept her virginity intact? Had she? Her good morality and integrity? She tried her best to keep these principles and ideals, but she struggled at times.

At daybreak, Geraldine was awake. She sat on a chair in front of her dressing table mirror. She was in a lethargic state, and caught sight of her reflection. She was narcissistic and full of self-love. Geraldine wanted to remain alone in her bedroom, which shone with a dim light. From her fantasies and dreams, she desired a romance.

Suddenly, her father came into her bedroom to check on his daughter.

"Now what?" grimaced Geraldine.

"You were on the phone for ages. You just natter on and on," answered her father.

"Did I? I didn't mean to," Geraldine grinned.

"Your mother does it well," said her father, complimenting his wife, "but you, you just natter. One of these days you're going to get yourself in trouble, you really are," he warned.

"I don't mean to, it's not intentional. My friends do say I rabbit on," Geraldine's cheeks flushed.

Her father pointed his finger at her, "Well, then you must do something about it. You haven't done so. It can't continue. It mustn't!"

Geraldine understood the implications of what her father was saying.

"I mustn't keep chatting," she said cautiously.

"With all these lawsuits and libel cases going on," said her father emphatically, "something must be done."

Geraldine was flustered, "What do you suggest?" she asked anxiously.

Her father stood in front of her as she sat at the dressing table. He put his finger to his lips, "Shush," and then burst out of his daughter's boudoir.

Geraldine stayed in her boudoir and remained seated. She thought about how she talked too much. A complete chatterbox on the phone. Generally she was a good talker and communicator, a potential negotiator with a great disposition at her disposal.

22

A Vacation / Business Trip

For Geraldine there had been certain times of trouble and turmoil. Geraldine and her family would go abroad and stay at a friend's house, a hotel, or a resort (depending on which season each particular vacation took place.)

Geraldine liked her times of peace, quiet and solitude. She greatly cherished it. To her it was something uniquely precious that she didn't want to take for granted.

The passengers all travelled from different time zones, going abroad to European or Caribbean locations. Their destination was mainly the Caribbean, as it was hot on the exotic, sultry islands. They always love the hot, sunny weather. Whether on vacation or business, Geraldine, her colleagues, and her family would normally stay at an island resort. Sometimes they would lounge on white, sandy beaches with palm trees. It was their favourite destination. Their preferred resort was an exotic, tropical one, with its thatched roof huts, tropical beach, bars and restaurants. They spent their hot days on the lovely beaches. Geraldine, her colleagues and her mother would sun themselves on the sand. The weather in the tropics was indeed lovely! At other times they would spend time together relaxing and lounging about, without encountering any intrusion or having their privacy invaded.

On tropical nights and days they all enjoyed their relaxation time, the spas, and the recreation and leisure facilities. The typical nightlife featured the Caribbean zest for life, with calypso music, drums, and percussion playing in the background.

23

Geraldine Reads French History (From Uprising to Revolution: A Paradoxical One)

During the late evening, Geraldine went alone into the study. She sat down on a swivel chair in front of an office desk. On top of the desk was a reference book and a history textbook. A cabinet door left open revealed a set of encyclopaedias on the bottom shelf. Geraldine read many pages of the history textbook. A historical account of Marie Antionette, a French queen. She tried to familiarise herself with French history. She had read about the French Revolution before.

Geraldine's father entered the study to find his daughter engrossed in the history textbook.

"Haven't you already read this by now?" he asked.

Geraldine had been disturbed by her father and lost her concentration, "Oh yes! I have!I am trying to familiarise myself with this part of French history," she replied.

The proud father looked admiringly at his daughter, "What exactly are you reading?" he asked.

"It's quite ironic. I guess I'm comparing living in society today. I sort of relate to it in some way. With regards to being an aristocrat with a heritage of aristocracy. The French queen Marie Antoinette lived a life of untold riches, while the hungry mob stormed the grand palace. The ill-fated queen ordered her servants to give them cake. Did the mob eat only crumbs? Anyway, the mob got the queen executed! A guillotine was used, which is pretty disturbing by all accounts. Death by guillotine! A queen beheaded! The mob were pleased that their queen was beheaded by a guillotine."

Geraldine's father was impressed by her knowledge, "You certainly do know your history. I am impressed!" he said proudly.

Geraldine admitted her difficulties and conditions that made it hard to cope. "At times I certainly can't come to terms with being an aristocrat. Am I the only one going through this? Perhaps others live an aristocratic life much better than I do. I dread it. I just want to hide and keep on hiding!"

"You can't keep hiding, you have to face it. Aristocracy is a reality. My Geraldine, one day you will be a countess married to an earl," predicted her father.

"Good heavens! Me? Never!" doubted Geraldine.

Her father had no doubt, "It is inevitable you will get married. A countess!" he said.

"Not me," tutted Geraldine.

The proud father smiled at his daughter who still sat at the desk. He touched her gently and then left the study, leaving her alone in the dimly lit study with its single lamp.

Geraldine was disturbed by the French history textbook, it alarmed her and caused her fear. She shuddered. The French revolution resulted in the beheading of a queen!

24

Geraldine Goes to Confession

Geraldine attended confession. She went into the confessional box where confessors confess to the priest. Geraldine, a sinner, had been redeemed. She repented of her sins. Her confessional experience was a deeply spiritual one.

The next day at her colleague's home, Geraldine blabbed about her confessional experience while sitting in the nice warm lounge. She enjoyed the heat from the radiators and the fire.

"As you were saying, what was it like?" her colleague, Sandra, was asking.

"You mean my confession? Oh! That! It was something I didn't plan, it just happened. I guess by a miracle. Or by chance," she paused.

"This confession, what's the point of it?" asked Sandra.

Geraldine acknowledged Sandra and admitted the confessional was a spiritual experience and encounter.

"It's really of a spiritual nature, that's what!" replied Geraldine.

"Isn't your family decadent? asked Sandra.

"I don't know. I guess they are. I can only speak for myself," answered Geraldine.

"Has this confession really made any difference to your life?" wondered Sandra.

Geraldine thought of the spiritual implication which was implicit in her deep contemplation, "In the long run it will have some effect and meaning. That I am positive about. A believer who truly does believe is a good thing."

"It is good, if you say so. If you believe in it, this religion," said Sandra positively.

"It is good. It is necessary to go to confession," said Geraldine unashamedly.

"With all that's going on in the world, you need faith and a religion," said Sandra.

"It is good to be religious, I think? Don't you?"

"Quite."

"With my confession, there may as well not be any more confessions going on in the future," said Geraldine.

"Well, I think if they are offering to provide it, well, one should go."

Geraldine reflected on her religious experience in the confessional box at the chapel and said yes, "I agree. That's why I took the opportunity to go to confession."

"Rather you than me," said Sandra.

"It is a good thing. Well, It's damn better than being a crackpot throwing crockery. There, there is peace. Going to confession in a quiet chapel is a peaceful scenario," smiled Geraldine.

"My beliefs may differ from yours to some extent. I don't know quite what to believe. I am in two minds about it," said Sandra apathetically.

Geraldine showed a willingness to go to confession, whereas Sandra was apathetic about the idea of attending a confessional at a chapel with an assigned priest.

25

Geraldine's Lonely Times

At times, Geraldine actually liked being alone. For her it was such a good feeling. She preferred it that way, and liked to keep away from people; her friends, acquaintances, and family members. It was a usual tendency of hers. She had an inclination to liking and having her own privacy. At times like this, Geraldine didn't want her family, friends or colleagues intruding or imposing on her, and invading her privacy.

Geraldine was intolerant of people being intrusive and obtrusive. She disliked them imposing on her, making impossible demands and requests. Whenever Geraldine had any turmoil, problems, difficulties, worries or anxieties, she tended to elude and avoid people.

Geraldine spent the weekend mainly being housebound. She had been called lonely, vigilant, wise and sensible. From time to time she was labelled a loner. She enjoyed her luxuries, comforts, pleasures, freedom, privacy and quietude though; and she had hedonistic tendencies.

Heraldine sometimes just kept away from everyone all weekend - which was something she did constantly.

It was a trait of hers. At home, Geraldine liked to spend days and nights alone indoors.

26

Geraldine's Wish and Desire to be an Ordinary Citizen

Geraldine wanted to relinquish the aristocracy and her aristocratic way of life. She wanted to be an ordinary citizen, just like everybody else. She disliked her aristocratic lifestyle.

Wanting and desiring a future change in her life for the better, Geraldine didn't want to live among the privileged classes as an aristocrat. The lifestyle didn't suit her. She just wanted that life to end, and to begin a new one. Relinquishing her life was preferable to her than living life as an aristocrat.

Her family lived the aristocratic lifestyle much better than she did. Their lifestyle was hedonistic in nature. Generally, most of the time, Geraldine lived a good way of life. She had a good lifestyle. But for Geraldine, she would rather live a common and ordinary life like the general populace!

Quite recently, Geraldine and her family had planned to go away again. This time, Geraldine and her family were going to escape to a country residence - an aristocratic one. Wallington Residence.

27

Heritage, Estates and Legacies

Geraldine, an aristocrat, often travelled to certain grand estates in various counties around the country. She was quite accustomed to it, as it was a characteristically aristocratic thing to do.

Geraldine was used to wealth, riches and affluence, greed and extravagance. Geraldine knew earls, duchesses, landowners, and aristocratic families. As an informed aristocrat, Geraldine was well-aware of legacies, restates and estates. It was common knowledge; all aristocrats knew. Aristocrats owning land and estates is an aristocratic custom and tradition. Practically every aristocrat and their family had followed suit.

Geraldine visited estate after estate. Geraldine was privileged. Aristocrats gained special priorities, but Geraldine in particular was prioritised over all of the others who were invited. Geraldine loved to visit the estates, whether invited alone or with family. It was a habitual, cultural tradition and a custom amongst members of the aristocracy. Geraldine visited imposing estates and admired the grand buildings. In particular she loved the delightful luxury rooms with adjacent bathrooms, the fine decor, furnishings, antiques, art, and the many many acres of land and gardens.

On occasion, Geraldine and her family would be invited to dinner or tea at an estate. Tea time in particular was a special time for Geraldine, she loved having a nice way in an authentic way, with a teapot and a tea cosy, china teacups and saucers. Visiting grand estates remained a personal custom and tradition for Geraldine and her family.

Earls, landowners, globists, populists, and tycoons didn't daunt Geraldine in any way, as she was so used to them. She was well-aware of any peril, risks, danger and threats. With security and personal bodyguards assigned, Geraldine could feel at ease. Geraldine was always alert and vigilant everytime she went to an estate, either with or without her family.

With great pride, Geraldine knew how increasingly popular culture and heritage seemed to be with the general public. Every season, tourists and visitors would also visit these grand venues. Admission to the estates was popular with sightseers. They flock back again and again. Beautifully uniformed guides were assigned to welcome them and offer guided tours of the properties.

28

A Teatime Special

Geraldine and her family had tea together in a nice, cosy living room. The aristocratic family sat together in front of a luxury fireplace. The logs crackled, burning in the fire, warming them all up. Her aunt, an experienced brewer from a tea company, leant over, and with a steady hand poured tea from a chocolate-brown, porcelain teapot into every cup on the silver tray.

Together they all drank the refreshing tea, and ate cupcakes and sandwiches. Geraldine liked the nice sweet tea very much. She took such joyful pleasure in the teatime. It was another good feeling, as only a few of her family members worked for an exclusive tea company. Geraldine's aunt was a great brewer, and made tea of the finest quality. Tea-making and brewing was her aunt's speciality. She had a natural skill for it and was obsessed with fresh tea bags. Geraldine's aunt was constantly fussy with regards to tea, with the process of making it. She was meticulous, and liked tea made in a certain way, using steam and boiling percolated water, purified in a luxury coffee maker.

All of them sat together by the fire in the dark, shadowy living room, the glowing embers flickering.

The satisfied tea-drinkers all took such joy and delight in drinking the nice tea prepared by Geraldine's aunt.

29

City Life

Geraldine had never been employed in the city. She had fears about the city with regards to crime and fraud, which was on the rise in society. Geraldine also feared being assaulted. However, she did desire to work in the city, especially as only a few of her family members had ever worked in the city. Geraldine did live in the city from time to time though… did she like it, or dislike it?

Geraldine was accustomed to the city lifestyle; she both liked and dreaded it! She had given up hope of ever working in the city, or indeed of ever considering working for an employer. The actual work environment and conditions were unfavourable to Geraldine, and she disapproved of them. Geraldine thought of herself as being too vulnerable, hypersensitive and exposed from being in a weak condition.

With her mind assailed, Geraldine suffered from fear and phobias yet again (she always tended to have fears. For instance the fear of an assailant assaulting her!) At times Geraldine was fearful. It made her feel exhausted and fatigued. As a fashion designer there had been many instances when she had nearly collapsed or fainted from being overworked, but at present she was apathetic about city life in general.

Occasionally, Geraldine disliked the bustling city life without question. As a dweller, Geraldine was cautious about pollution emissions and crime in the city (her family used security and bodyguards.) Additionally, Geraldine took self-defence classes due to the threat of being attacked - her family too!

In the past, Geraldine had been haunted by her phobias. The thought of getting attacked crossed her mind constantly - so for her and her family, staying safe was a priority. The self-defence classes made a difference to them all. It made them tough, strong, formidable and invincible to some extent.

Personally, Geraldine preferred to escape to the country, as it was where she felt most at home.

30

Legacy

(A Generational Thing)

Recently, an aristocrat had died; Squire Lord Hunting. A private family funeral took place.

At home, during the weekend, Geraldine sat with her mother in the living room. The downstairs room was much warmer than any of the other rooms in the detached house. Geraldine sat next to her mother on the couch. Her impatient mother at once informed her daughter about the outcome of Lord Hunting's testate.

"Lord Hunting's estate will be available for the public to visit."

"Yes. What about his possessions, and those sorts of things?" asked Geraldine concernedly.

"It gets passed on," replied her mother.

"What! To this generation?" gasped Geraldine.

"Oh yes, with certainty," said her mother.

Geraldine spoke softly, "Rather them than me."

Her self-opinionated mother spoke about it briefly, concluding, "It's really no surprise to me that the estate is going to be open to the public. I sort of expected it. It's nothing new. And after all, it is a tradition, a generational thing, isn't it?"

Geraldine's mood changed (hers was an erratic one), and she sat up from the couch and walked towards the door, leaving her mother alone in the living room. Geraldine went upstairs to her bedroom, and there she reflected on the late squire, Lord Hunting, his passing, his funeral, and his legacy.

A few days before, Geraldine had stayed at her uncle's home, a large country manor. She spent her time in the large kitchen, sitting with her parents at the kitchen table. Her aunt made her a cordial drink and cheese and cucumber (thinly sliced) sandwich. Arriving late at her uncle's, Geraldine felt dazed from feeling dozy, tired, lethargic and sluggish. Geraldine got irritated at them for talking too long, and she felt moody. Geraldine got up from the pine chair, and slid it back under the kitchen table with the other empty chairs.

In a moody state, she left the kitchen, which was cooling down thanks to an extractor and an electric fan. Slowly she made her way to the dining room, where she expected to find her nephew, Cyril, sitting in a chair at the dining table. He was eating fresh caviar and a handful of pork scratchings.

"Do join me. Sit down," said her nephew.

Geraldine stayed standing, with both her arms folded gracefully, "Yes, I can see you do like it," she said.

"It's not fat porkies. Yes. I do. I like it very much. Want some?" gestured Cyril.

Geraldine was amused at his wit, "Me! No! No thanks. I must watch my diet. My figure."

Cyril took notice of Geraldine's figure, admiring the sight of it, "You look alright to me," he shrugged. "What's the problem?"

"Nothing. I'm on a diet. I have to watch my calories, don't I," said Geraldine.

"If you say so. Your figure always looks alright to me."

Geraldine remembered some really fine occasions when they were invited as dinner guests, "Yes, we've had some really good feasts," she said.

"Yes, Debbie is a good cook, isn't she?" said Cyril admiringly.

"She sure is, that's for sure. I do miss it when Debbie doesn't cook for us," pined Geraldine.

Cyril admitted that too, and his emotion showed it, "I do too," he said. "Debbie just doesn't have the time for us, has she?"

"I'm afraid not," sighed Geraldine.

Both Geraldine and Cyril admired how well Debbie could cook. She was a professional cook and an epicure.

She was a professional at oriental cookery, with an admirable style.

31

Mothers Attending Church Creche With an Odd Parent

Due to a change in Geraldine's situation, she had to change her usual plans, and so she went to church on a Monday morning. (Geraldine already suffered from a trauma, and she was now traumatised from another situation, and had no control over what was happening to her.)

During the morning, Geraldine attended church. At that time there was a creche, and so she joined mothers with their children, babies, toddlers and infants. Some mothers took refuge there in order to suit themselves. There were many prams inside the church itself, and there was a designated area mainly for toddlers and their mothers.

Geraldine joined the mothers, all sitting together in one area. One of the seated mothers spoke calmly while holding and feeding her baby.

"They are not exactly aristocrats, are they?" she was asking.

"No, they are not. Simply just ordinary," replied Geraldine.

Geraldine personally took sanctuary inside the church too. She observed while standing near to the altar, the colourful stained glass windows which depicted apostles and saints.

Geraldine attended the church sometimes. She was a contemplator who liked the peace, quiet and sanctuary inside the church. Certain mothers also came here sometimes to seek refuge themselves. Some of the mothers just came for the creche, and to be somewhere with their infants and other mothers.

32

Geraldine Deeply Misses the Grandchildren

Unfortunately, due to separation, Geraldine hadn't seen any of the grandchildren for ages (it had been quite a long time since the families had met), and they had also moved away, and were now living overseas.

Geraldine often thought of them and wondered about them. Geraldine was deeply attached to the grandchildren, and always kept in touch with them regularly. They would phone Geraldine, or she would phone them. At times they exchanged messages on the answering machine. Their conversations, whether long or short, were always affectionate, sweet, and sentimental. There was a deep fondness and love between all of them. They all eagerly hoped to meet up and see eachother again soon. They looked forward to the next time they would meet up and be together. They all desired and wished for this to happen!

Constantly they wished to be together again. The affectionate families were hopeful and optimistic about coming back together again quite soon. Just like real, loving families should!

33

A Swiss Break

When stopping at the border of Switzerland, Geraldine and her family stayed at a luxury hotel for two nights. In the foyer were columns and pillars near the reception, where there was a linguistic receptionist on duty.

Geraldine and her family sat near a fireplace. These holidaymakers enjoyed the peace, quiet, calm and solace as they kept themselves warm by the heat of the log fire. They all took comfort from the warmth and luxury. There was such peace, quiet, privacy, solitude and quietude, as well as luxurious, sumptuous surroundings of the highest standard.

While the family relaxed, they heard a melodic sound; a glockenspiel, or perhaps a music box, seemingly coming from the luxurious lounge. The delightful melody resonated with the melodious sound of bells ringing and brass. The family sitting in armchairs in front of the fire felt calm, relaxed and happy, as well as peaceful. As time passed, more guests appeared in the foyer of the hotel. Some guests checked in at reception, while others went into the bar, lounge, or restaurant to dine. Diners dined at their reserved tables, attended to by the restaurateur.

Geraldine was with some of the grandchildren. Earlier they had been reunited and reconciled after the period of separation. Leaving her parents alone in the seating area of the foyer, Geraldine walked, with the grandson and granddaughter following behind. They caught up with Geraldine and together they headed in the direction of the endless corridors, where hotel rooms were numbered according to section. Each section had an entrance and exit, so guests staying in each particular section could arrive and leave easily. They saw a foursome of guests walking down the corridor.

Geraldine and the grandchildren reached her plush hotel room which was at the end of a very long corridor at the end of one section. Geraldine used her door pass and tapped it on the hotel door. The door opened automatically. Together they all entered the hotel room. The excited grandchildren admired the lovely room.

"Wow, isn't it grand!" exclaimed Katie.

"Yeah! Wow!" said the grandson excitedly.

Standing with her arms crossed, Geraldine asked the excitable grandchildren to keep their voices down. She put a finger to her pouty lips, and pressed it firmly to her lips, which had beautifully applied red lipstick.

"Shush," she said.

Geraldine heard the wind blowing outside. She was overwhelmed by the awe of nature and the elements. She too marvelled at the sight of her hotel room,

"Isn't it just fabulous? I just can't wait!"

Geraldine turned her attention to the little guests who had joined her in her hotel room. Standing close to them she felt overwhelmed with emotion, and embraced them both affectionately.

"At least we are together," she said beatifically. "It's so good to be back together."

"Yes! We are!"

"Hurrah!"

After they had all spent a short time in Geraldine's hotel room, they left and made their way back to the lounge, where their parents were waiting for tea. The luxury suite had fine lighting that was bright and beautiful.

Day and night the family spent time together at the luxury five-star hotel, making full use of all the facilities, amenities and provisions available - including room service. They ended up staying for several days and nights, showing such love, affection, respect, fondness and regards towards each other. They all stayed together in luxurious comfort, using the bar and restaurant, as well as staying in their quiet rooms where they could enjoy solitude. Ultimately, this all lasted for a day and two nights.

34

Geraldine and Her Parents Visit Mr and Mrs Sturges at their Country Manor Home (A Greek Mythology)

On a cold Thursday afternoon, Geraldine and her parents came to stay at Mr and Mrs Sturges's home; a beautiful country manor. At that time, during mid-afternoon, Geraldine and her mother, along with Mr and Mrs Sturges, sat together in an insulated, nice and warm conservatory, with various house plants and lovely flower pots everywhere. It really looked beautiful, with tropical and exotic plants in terracotta pots.

Outside, the thick heavy raindrops splattered onto the glass panes of the tropical conservatory. Geraldine's chatty mother talked with Mrs Sturges while Geraldine took the initiative to the professional and cultured Mr Sturges (an eccentric, inquisitive and studious archeologist.)

"Well, can you tell me, Mr Sturges, whether you have recently discovered anything new in that excavation of yours?" enquired Geraldine.

"Oh yes! We have found relics on one site. I can't really say what or where - for obvious reasons - but I can tell you that we have excavated a vase that we believe to be ancient Greek," answered Mr Sturges.

Geraldine had been inquisitive, and listened to Mr Sturges with a curious fascination. He told her about his archaeology, and she was admirably impressed at his findings and discoveries.

"Oh how fascinating! Your archaeology must take you all over the world. All those expeditions and excavations!" said Geraldine.

The deeply thoughtful archaeologist said, "At another site in the east, we have excavated ancient relics and pieces, and elsewhere a colleague of mine discovered a tapestry. A historian came down to take a look."

"Egyptology sounds so mysterious, strange and sinister. I don't know what to make of it. It is idolatry," assumed Geraldine.

"With Egyptology and dark pyramids, it is dark, cryptic, and sinister in most cases. It is ancient history dating back to an ancient era."

"Do you like Egypt?" Geraldine asked him.

"For us archaeologists, Egypt is, in essence, a root. Our main source and foundation in general for all of our work; our expeditions, excavations and new discoveries."

Geraldine was ignorant about archaeology. She seldom showed interest in anything unless she was fascinated by it. "I guess it must be," she said thoughtfully.

"Do you take an interest in archaeology?" asked Mr Sturges. "You really ought to, it's fascinating."

"No, not really. It's something I don't know much about, but it must be fascinating," said Geraldine.

"My lovely wife helps with the expeditions," said Mr Sturges.

"That's jolly good! How nice!"

Mr Sturges instructed Geraldine to get some knowledge about the subject, and told her to take a look at some archaeology programmes.

"Oh I will do that!I certainly will," said Geraldine assuredly.

The enervated husband kissed his wife and, feeling tired and exhausted, left her alone with their guests. Mr Sturges took time to rest, relaxing in an armchair alone in another room and smoking a pipe.

Geraldine and her mother rested and relaxed for another hour, and eventually their chauffeur arrived to drive them back home. Their journey back was a long one.

35

Jetset

Geraldine was a jetsetter from a jetsetting family. They stayed at five-star hotels all over the world. They were well-accustomed to hoteliers and restaurateurs, of course. The odd member of Geraldine's family had now retired from public duties and engagements.

Nowadays, Geraldine, an aristocrat, tends to isolate herself from everyone - including her family. Avoiding and eluding them was just something she did sometimes. Geraldine took joy and pleasure in having her freedom, peace, silence, quietude and solitude; without any restrictions or limitations imposed or enforced on her. Geraldine was much happier being free and single, alone, secluded, and isolated. She preferred things that way than any other. Usually she was peaceful, placid and happy living in seclusion. Geraldine loved her freedom and quietude, as well as her peace and solitude.

In the past, this had been difficult for Geraldine, for she was once a young aristocrat growing up. When she was younger she had been naive and unsophisticated, vulgarian and vulnerable, exposed, and discontented at times about her adolescence and the period of womanhood. For Geraldine, life changed for the better as she matured and gained experience in life from daily living.

Geraldine delighted in all of her exciting and wonderful memories and joyful, thrilling experiences. She called and reminisced about her past.

Now, Geraldine's life within the aristocracy had changed. She was much more of an ordinary person - a European or British citizen - rather than an aristocrat. As Geraldine was a freelance fashion designer by profession, she was obsessed with designing new fashion collections (including garments and outfits.)

For Geraldine, this obsession was a compulsion she'd had since working retail. As it stood, Geraldine's aristocratic life had taken a twist. Her life now was simply common and pretty ordinary, and her hectic lifestyle had become less and less glamorous.

Ultimately, the jetset and glamour had just faded away. Recalling it now, it was just something of a past memory. A reminiscence of evocative memories…

Epilogue

Geraldine, an aristocrat, dreams and desires a handsome earl. She is destined to be a countess. But is that really her destiny? Geraldine romanticised about the earl. His wealth, riches, fortune, good looks, estate… and his horses, of course.

Geraldine wondered if the earl truly fancied her. Did he desire her? She often dreamt of a romance with him. A landowner, horseman, and a squire. She even wondered if she would ever get a chance to ride any of the fine horses that he owned.

With a girlish envy she desired to own a palomino stallion, and Arabian horses. Isn't it every girl's dream to own a horse of her own?! (Two members of her family owned horses, thoroughbreds of their own.)

Geraldine's friends were riders themselves. These good riders and horsewomen have equestrian possession, territory and control themselves when they ride out into the fields and the vast wilderness.

Geraldine The Loner (A Lonesome Aristocrat)

Geraldine, under the circumstances, knew she should consider relinquishing being an aristocrat by actually being a normal person and living in poverty. She did wonder if she should do that with serious consideration to the aristocracy. Her displeasure was absolutely made clear to all of those who knew her. Those alert observers were fully aware of Geraldine's passionate outbursts of contempt against the aristocracy.

For Geraldine, the status that came with being a member of the aristocracy was unappealing and caused her apathy. She was apathetic about the stratum in general, for the aristocracy and for her. Keeping up with the aristocracy's ideologies, ethics, traditions and customs, made her feel indifferent and apathetic. Depending on the situation, Geraldine would normally meet or come across other aristocrats, though it would depend if it was in her interest to be with any of them. Preferably she would be with her favourite loved ones, or perhaps a heart's desire.

Otherwise, Geraldine would usually avoid and elude them. Especially those in which she had no particular interest at all. Outsiders, newcomers, and guests of latecomers would all be evidently cautious and wary of Geraldine's situation. At the present time, Geraldine would suit herself and stay at home. She preferred it that way, and so day after day she isolated herself indoors.

She avoided and eluded her family, friends, acquaintances and guests at times.

A Getaway (An Absconder and Jetsetter)

On one occasion, Geraldine applied makeup beautifully well. It accentuated her features. Geraldine dressed up, looking lovely. She left the house with her family. They travelled to the main train station in central London, and they boarded the fast train for the airport. Once they had attended to their luggage and had gone through passport control, the family relaxed in the airport together and ate lunch.

During the course of the day, the passengers looked up at the monitor, hoping for their gate number to show. Finally it appeared. Flashing on the screen: their gate number. Quickly Geraldine and her family made their way to their gate. They waited in the departure lounge.

They lined up to show the uniformed officials their passports, then they hurried to board the plane, heading from London to the south of France. After a short flight, they landed at their scheduled time. Arriving at the airport, Geraldine and her family had their passports checked and then collected their luggage from the conveyor belt. The other passengers followed suit.

Standing in the entrance of the airport, the family waited for their taxi. After a considerable time, their taxi arrived. They hurried to get in. finally they reached their destination of a continental hotel.

Since that momentous time, Geraldine had never looked back. She ended up residing with her family in a luxury penthouse in the south of France, in a providence region. The family all had a fabulous time.

For Geraldine and her family it was more or less a perfect getaway and escape from their dull life in England in the English countryside.

Intimate Monaco Experiences

Geraldine loved Monaco, supposedly one of the richest countries in the world. It was a millionaire's paradise for the rich and wealthy, playboys, the jetset, and the elite. Geraldine had empathy with them; she related to the jetset, elite and stratum. She liked it here. Better than anywhere else in Europe.

In Monaco Geraldine had freedom, peace, joy and happiness. Where else in the world could she find such joy, pleasure, peace and love? Nowhere else. It was undeniable. Geraldine indeed did love the highlife on this glamorous continent. She loved the nightlife, the entertainment, the food and drink, and also the shopping in all of the fashion boutiques. Shopping was an obsession of hers - a typical woman!

Geraldine and her family liked to dine out in style. They were members of an exclusive sports and fitness club. They used the gymnasium, spa and swimming pool, as well as the other amenities and facilities. Individual members of Geraldine's family were also members of a yacht and sailing club, and went on a luxury catamaran out on the calm sea.

For Geraldine and her family, finding true freedom, peace, bliss and happiness was the best thing they had ever experienced in their lives. They adored this country.

Geraldine: A Recluse

One afternoon, Geraldine spent hours doing fine dressmaking. During that time, she felt a sharp pain and realised she had broken her fingernail. She felt a pain in her cuticle and discomfort. So Geraldine ended up not working anymore that day, or the next.

Geraldine stayed in the living room and relaxed and rested. She spent the time sitting on the sofa in front of the fireplace. She relaxed and took comfort in the warmth of the room, and luxuriated in a graceful position. She took joy and delight in being comfortable, and she liked even more being all alone in silence.

Sometimes Geraldine preferred being alone, without being in the presence of any of her family, friends or colleagues, and without guests coming to see her. She didn't like people imposing upon her or intruding on her privacy yet again, time after time.

At times Geraldine would keep away from all of them. She avoided and eluded them. She made up excuses, which they often objected to. Did this alienate them? At times and in certain situations, yes. But Geraldine remained selfish, unconcerned, indifferent, moody, temperamental and an eluder! Geraldine liked her privacy even more than ever before. She stayed indoors, remaining in these conditions.

Geraldine, a dressmaker and fashion designer, spent less time than usual dressmaking or designing new, elaborate patterns and dress designs. Did she live the life of a recluse? Did she relinquish the life of an aristocrat? Geraldine's aristocratic lifestyle was no longer a typical, customary, aristocratic one. Geraldine spent less and less time going to events and functions. They became more and more infrequent and she ended up being something of a hermit by staying constantly indoors, or with close friends at their homes.

PART THREE

Geraldine's Brother, Greg

1

The End of Summer Term

Greg went to his form room to attend registration. He sat down on the left hand side of the table. A school fellow nudged him with his elbow,

"You're telling porkies," said Don.

"It's the truth, honest," said Greg.

Another school fellow sitting next to him pointed his finger at him, remaining calm.

"You lie," said Don.

Greg denied it. Pete, in disgust, got up from his chair. He sat somewhere else at the table in another chair.

During registration, the tutor read out their names. Every form member acknowledged their name being called out by the form tutor. After registration, a few of the pupils began to give out Christmas cards. Greg was unhappy and miserable because he received no Christmas cards from anyone in his form. Greg hated them. He was unappreciative of their thoughtlessness. He had disrespect and disregard for them. He had resentment for the whole form.

Greg was unconcerned about not receiving any Christmas cards. His form was selfish and inconsiderate. Greg felt unloved this Christmas. No one even shared their seasonal greetings. In previous school years, Greg had only received a few cards, and the ones given to him were pretty cheap. Greg envied how certain individuals received many Christmas cards. He was envious of those who received a large number of Christmas cards! In comparison, he had only ever received a few. He was embarrassed by the constant rejection; the response of rejection he received from everybody.

At the end of registration, the form attended their lessons as usual. All of the classes ran as normal, except for periods five and six. At that time there was an end of term assembly. In another building, the whole form attended the assembly in the school hall. The headmaster, who was wearing a mohair suit, addressed the pupils. He congratulated the school for a successful school year. The headmaster wanted to emulate the previous school year, and had surpassed it with academic excellence.

Greg was pleased that school had finally ended. It was the end of the summer term. The end of his third year at state school.

2

Christmas at Home

During the Christmas holidays, Greg stayed at home with his depressive mother (his mother was a single parent and suffered from arthritis.) Greg's family neglected him, and uninvited him from their homes at Christmastime (only for the short period of the Christmas festivities), and so Christmas was a depressing time for Greg and his mother.

Greg opened his Christmas presents at another time. These unwanted gifts were probably quite cheap and ordinary. On Christmas Day, at dawn, Greg sneaked downstairs to open his presents which were under the Christmas tree. The tree lights flashed on and off. The shining brilliance of the varied-coloured Christmas lights dazzled.

Greg was ungrateful for the presents which he received. A got a jumper, a toy sports car, a children's book (limited edition), and a stocking which had a selection of chocolates inside. Much earlier, Mrs Henning had been disturbed by her son sneaking downstairs. Mrs Henning, who was already dressed, came downstairs, wondering if her son was excited about Christmas. A child's excitement at Christmas was wonderful! Mrs Henning grinned like a childish girl.

Greg grinned when he was intruded upon by his mother. His mischievousness was like a naughty schoolboy.

Mr Henning opened her Christmas presents. She tore open the Christmas wrapping paper. Mrs Henning received a new pot, table cloths, and a tin of biscuits. She opened the tin of luxury assorted chocolate biscuits, and offered one to her son. Mrs Henning decided to make cups of tea. Her romantic notion charmed Greg.

"I know, let's make a cup of tea and have biscuits," said Mrs Henning.

"Hey, that's a good idea," smiled her son.

Greg got up from a kneeling position and straightened up. He stretched his legs which ached from a cramp, and sat down in a lounge chair. He ate a chocolate shortbread biscuit. He nibbled at the layer of milk chocolate, taking joyful delight in eating the biscuit. About a quarter of an hour later, Mrs Henning came back into the living room. She carried a tray with two mugs of tea on it.

Greg and his mother spent time together drinking tea and eating luxury biscuits, much to their satisfied delight. For Greg, eating chocolate biscuits was like an aphrodisiac - he had a real liking for Swiss and Belgian chocolate.

Greg stayed up for about an hour. As soon as he became tired, he left his mother and went back to bed.

He recovered, and slept for the remaining time that was left to sleep.

On another day, Greg and his mother watched a film on television. The long film had been edited to a short, European version. Mrs Henning was sentimental, emotional, soppy and romantic. This nostalgic film remained one of her favourites. Greg thought the film was iconic and nostalgic because of its significant Christmas theme. One of the actors starring in it was a legend. The supporting actors and actresses were great too!

During the film, Mrs Henning impulsively ate some milk and dark chocolates from a tray of a box of chocolates. Greg had been allowed to eat only a few chocolates. His mother was pretty selfish, refusing him to take any more chocolates from the box.

Of course, Greg tried to understand the meaning and significance of the film. Peace had been declared. Greg realised it was about peacetime at Christmas. During the remaining hours of the day, Greg lounged about, enjoying his freedom and pleasurable relaxation at Christmas. His mother enjoyed her free time alone in her bedroom.

The next day, Terry, Greg's brother, played with toy soldiers in his bedroom. Greg and Terry made sounds of rapid machine gun fire. Every time they fired, they each knocked down a soldier. They took it in turns to fire at each other's soldiers. The one who knocked down the most, won the game of war. The commanders knocked down more soldiers than the German army. During the game, they must have lost a soldier when putting them all back in the tin.

Terry painted the soldiers. He was quite good at it. He painted them in intricate detail. It was admirable how he did it. He used various paints to paint the soldiers, fighters, and bombers. Up on the ceiling, the painted fighters and bombers hung down. All painted in camouflage colours.

Later in the afternoon, Greg and Terry sat at the dining table in the dining room. It was decorated with Christmas decorations. They ate a roast Christmas dinner and a Christmas pudding. Later, their mother treated them to a strawberry milkshake made with fresh strawberries and milk. Greg and Terry appreciated their mother's treat. They both drank the fresh milkshake from a tumbler.

Afterwards, Mrs Henning and Terry watched television. Greg stayed in his bedroom. He preferred to be alone. He enjoyed the peace and quiet. Greg realised that as soon as Christmas was over, his mother would begin to nag at him and his brother again (Greg's school report was rather bad!)

Greg preferred his privacy rather than being in the company of his mother and brother. At times, his older brother was annoying, and his angry mother was bitchy towards him. Greg lounged alone in his bedroom. He took enjoyment from his freedom, peace and quietude. Greg was meditative sitting alone in his bedroom, and was deeply contemplative. Greg did not do his homework, which was to read a classic novel for English Literature.

3

Greg's Disappointment

Greg came out of his bedroom and went downstairs. He joined his mother in the lounge. Mrs Henning was reading a magazine. His obsessive mother often occupied her time by reading columns.

"Greg, I would like a word. Your school report is bad. Your grades are bad. It's appalling. Your learning is shallow," said Mrs Henning.

"Mum, I have tried," groaned Greg.

"I send you to school to learn, not to mess about. You're a disgrace. You're doing badly at school. Get out of my sight! You make me sick! Go to your room this instant!" said his mother angrily.

Greg obeyed his mother. His temperamental mother was moody. He went back upstairs to his bedroom. He stayed in his room for a short time.

Greg had the urge to get out. He climbed out of his bedroom window and walked onto the flat roof. He walked to the side of the roof, and climbed down onto the wooden gate. He jumped down onto the ground. Greg went out of the front drive and made his way to the main highstreet. He headed to the public library and entered through the automatic doors. There he came across a French student alone in the children's section of the library. Greg began to chat up the French female student. The student wrote down her name and address on a piece of paper, and Greg left her - was she an au pair?

Greg walked back home. He wrote to the French student, and she responded with a letter. Greg wrote back. Unfortunately, the French student didn't write back again. Greg had been stood up while waiting to hopefully meet the French student. Greg was disappointed. Greg hated girls! He suffered from a phobia of them!

Greg stayed in his bedroom and sulked. He was very disappointed. About fifty minutes later, Mrs Henning came into her son's bedroom. She agitated her son, who was miserable and unhappy.

"Son, what's wrong? You're spending far too much time in your bedroom."

Greg scowled, "Everything is wrong," he moaned.

"Son, come down. You spend too much time in your bedroom."

Greg moved his hair out of his eyes and glared at his mother, "I am not telling you, mum. There is nothing to say."

"Don't be like that. I am only trying to help."

Mrs Henning left to go shopping, and Greg stayed longer in his bedroom. His bedroom was warmer than anywhere else in the cold house. Greg enjoyed the comfort of being alone in his bedroom. He overindulged, laying down on the comforting softness of his luxury mattress. He rested for about an hour. He recovered from his exhaustion and tiredness by staying in bed and resting.

4

Greg is Invited to a Party

Kerry drove Tina and her brother, Greg, to their friend's house. A party was being held there. They arrived at Tammy's house. Kerry parked the car outside the house. The driveway was full of parked cars. Kerry stood and rang the doorbell. A guest answered the front door. Kerry, Tina and Greg entered the house. Kerry and Tina were greeted by the welcomers. Greg remained unwelcomed.

Tina received a lot of attention from the other party guests, she was adored and admired. All the guests liked and loved Tina. She was well-loved by everyone. The guests were unfriendly to Greg. They snubbed, shunned and rejected him. The guests only paid attention to Kerry and Tina. The birthday girl came towards them. Tammy welcomed Kerry, Tina and Greg. Tammy embraced Tina and Kerry. She also greeted Greg with a hug. None of the other guests took any notice of him. The unfriendly guests were not welcoming to him.

Greg thought the guests were unpleasant and unfriendly. He stayed with his sister until she was led away by her friends. Greg found himself lost in the crowd. Some of the guests objected to him being invited; they disapproved of Tina's brother.

Later, the party guests all entered the dining room. There they ate a feast. Greg helped himself to a paper plate. He stood by himself in the far corner, eating sandwiches. Some of the girls at the party were pretty and attractive. A few others were ugly and unattractive. Greg did not desire the undesirable ones.

Losing his sister and her friend, Kerry, again, Greg found himself standing with all the females. None of them took heed of him. They took no notice of this lanky teenager with acne. He had been ignored and neglected again. They talked amongst themselves. It was a good conversation between female friends.

The dancing took place in the living room. The females all stood dancing, impressing each other with their dance moves. Greg joined them. He did his 'Action Man' dance routine. He enjoyed himself. The girls liked his dance; they were impressed by it. He danced with a boyish nature - in a teenage way.

After his dance, Greg decided to get out. He went out alone into the big garden. He felt lonely in the presence of females. None of them took any notice of him. Seemingly they preferred the company of their (female) friends.

Greg felt tired and exhausted after dancing so vigorously. He felt fatigued, especially as he had spent all of yesterday afternoon playing football with his brother. Greg was allowed to sit in a bedroom until it was time for his sister and her friend to leave the party.

Kelly was the driver, and she got them all home in about three quarters of an hour's time.

5

Greg's Deep Appreciation

Alone in his bedroom, Greg played with a train set. He watched the train going along the track around and around. Tina came in uninvited. Greg had been deeply reflective. He was engrossed in deep contemplation, and his sister disturbed him. Tina stood beside her brother, facing the track which ran around his bedroom. There was plenty of space in the large bedroom, even with furniture, a double bed and a wardrobe.

"Did you like the party?" asked Tina.

"Oh yes. I did like it. I wasn't going to go. Why did Tammy invite me?" asked Greg.

"Tammy likes you, she thinks you're cute," replied Tina.

Greg deeply appreciated the invite to Tammy's party. Tammy had given him a warm welcome, which he greatly appreciated.

"I didn't know anybody, apart from you two and a few others. The rest were strangers. The best part about the party was the dancing. I danced the night away. Everybody was sweet and lovely. I cherished every moment of it. I truly loved everyone. Personally, I thank Tammy for inviting me from the bottom of my heart. It ended up being quite a memorable night. I didn't expect that. Thank you for putting in a good word for me. I'd like to thank your friend, Kerry, for taking the time to drive me there and back. I had a good time, I really did," said Greg.

Standing up, Greg put his arm around his sister, feeling full of deep love and appreciation. He appreciated her consideration. Tina, his sweet sister, smiled with charm, and left her brother alone in his bedroom. Staring out of the window, Greg was lost in a daydream, watching the train go around the track in his bedroom.

Tina had left her brother's bedroom, and stood outside his door. She remembered what she had forgotten to do, and entered Greg's bedroom again.

"Oh yes," she said to him, "this is a note." She took out a piece of paper and began to read it aloud, "It's from my friend, Tammy, it says, *'Thank you, Greg, for coming to my party. My friends really liked you. They think you are a poet, a lyricist. I liked the words, especially these words:*

The Day That Never Came

The day that never came,
It did go and it did come.
It goes and it comes.
It leaves and it lasts.
It lingers and it fades.

These words you did show me. It kind of reminded me of an old Hollywood science fiction movie. You could be a poet, you are a lyricist in the making. Greg, do keep it up! My friends also liked your dancing. It was cool! Really cool dancing. I am sorry I could not talk to you at the end of my party. I'm afraid I can only apologise. At the time I was too busy. Everybody wanted attention. Anyway, I did sort them all out. I had no time for myself. I am glad you had a good time. Please, do come again. Maybe next time. Love Tammy, with kisses."

After Tina read the note, she folded the piece of paper and quickly left her brother's bedroom. Tina was rather satisfied and pleased with herself.

6

Greg's Deep Gratitude

Greg could not sleep that night, so he stayed up and decided to write a letter to Tammy. In appreciative acknowledgement of the invitation to her party, he wrote:

Dear Tammy,

It would please me if you do get this letter. Thank you, Tammy, for inviting me to your party. It really made my day. No one ever really invites me to their parties. So it was wonderful when you invited me to yours. I was surprised you did invite me. How you made allowances for me. You're a good friend of my sister, she must have put in a good word for me so that you would invite me.

Now about the party itself. The party was full of strangers. I did not know them. Nor did I know their names. They sort of tolerated me, even though they must have disapproved of me being invited to your party. I had an enjoyable time at your party. It was better than I imagined. My dancing went well. I did make an impression; people took notice of me. I shall always remember that night. It was something to remember.

Tammy, you were so sweet, friendly and considerate. Thank you very much for inviting me. It ended up being a wonderful night. One of my best nights.

Love, Greg

Greg put the note in an envelope and sealed it. He gave it to Tina the next time she went to Tammy's house, a few days later. Tammy read the note, sensing Greg's deep appreciation of the invitation to her party.

7

Tammy's Note

About a week later, on a Thursday afternoon, Greg was in his bedroom when suddenly something was pushed under his bedroom door. There he saw an envelope. It had been hand delivered. Greg picked the envelope up and opened it. To his surprise he found a note inside from Tammy. He read the note:

Dear Greg,

It was a pleasure to invite you to my party. You are welcome, even if my friends did object to you being invited. I will not tolerate that. I will sort them out. I don't think they all disapproved? Did they? I am glad you had a good time. My friends did like you. I like you. You were great fun. A joy to be with. I am glad you came to my party. You brightened up my day. Please feel free to talk to me. Let me know through your sister. You are welcome to come again, I really look forward to having you again.

Love, Tammy

Greg smelled the glorious scent of a luxury perfume. Was it perfumed? Whatever it was, it was ravishing and exquisite. Greg put the note back in the envelope and put it on his desk. After a while he forgot all about it, until he saw it on his desk and it reminded him. He took the note out again and took another look at it. He read it a few times.

8

Greg's Sister Spoke

It was late at night. Tina entered her brother's bedroom.

"Before I forget, can you shed any light on the party?" asked Greg.

"You mean the party we went to a couple of weeks ago?" replied Tina.

"Yes, that party."

"Tammy intended to invite many people. In the end, she only invited a certain number of people. I asked her if I could invite my brother. Tammy seemed enthusiastic about it, and she permitted me to. She allowed it. She allowed me to invite you to the party. The large number of people she had intended to invite, she did not. Tammy narrowed it down, and cut down the number of people she decided to give an invitation to.

Tammy received a large number of presents. She was blissful. Tammy personally thanked everyone. Tammy liked you. That's why she invited you. Giving an invitation to you was always her intention. Tammy didn't change her mind. Tammy loved celebrating her birthday with a party."

When his sister had finished speaking, Greg was starting to lose his patience. He showed his sister out of his bedroom. He was pleased with his considerate sister.

9

Peeping Tom

During the weekend, Greg got bored of staying in his bedroom alone. He spent an unexciting time there. In the afternoon he left his bedroom. He came downstairs and went out into the garden. He stopped at a tree. He climbed the tree. He climbed up the branches of the tree. He climbed higher and higher up the tree. Reaching the top of the tree, he kept still up in the branches.

From that high up in the tree, Greg got a view of the neighbours house, which faced directly opposite. Greg desired to take a peep at his neighbour. He looked through a bedroom window and saw a teenager dancing. Greg held a curious fascination for his neighbour. The female teenager had good looks. Greg became uneasy of being spotted all of a sudden by the teenager, so he stopped looking at his neighbour, due to unease and embarrassment.

He carefully lowered himself down from the tree, lower and lower, and reclined down the lowest part of the tree. He jumped down onto the ground. He landed safely. He got back up on his feet.

Greg, with awkward uncertainty, did not peek at his neighbour again. He did not climb the tree again either, it was too dangerous. He did not want to risk having a serious accident. Greg stayed in his bedroom and lounged about.

Later, his mother drove him to the supermarket to do the weekly shop. Hours later, on that Saturday afternoon, Greg went to the park with his friend to kick a football around. Greg was in the netted goal as a goalkeeper, making saves. His friend scored goals. They played for about an hour before eventually going home.

At home, Greg missed the football results on television. The football team he supported had lost again. It was now three successive defeats. Greg wore his football scarf and a cap. In disgust he took the cap off and threw it. Greg was disappointed that his team had been defeated at home, 1 - 0.

10

Greg's Last Memories

Greg was in the study reading an encyclopaedia. Suddenly, his sister Tina came into the study and disturbed him from reading.

"I'm sorry to tell you this," she said.

Greg, distracted from his sister entering the study, was startled, and closed the encyclopaedia, "What's up?" he asked.

"Clarice died."

Greg was deeply shocked, "Oh! How?" he asked.

"She was riding her horse when she fell. She was pronounced dead on arrival at the hospital."

"No! She can't be!" said Greg in disbelief.

"Clarice was a lovely friend of mine."

Greg recalled Tammy's party, "I remember at the party, Tammy was taking photos. Clarice was there with me. She didn't talk to me. She did not say anything to me. I just wanted to be with her. I desired her. I loved her," he said fondly.

Greg remembered that at the party they were photographed together. He remembered the chic, stunning redhead in the black dress, stockings, and black slip-on shoes. Clarice's makeup had been beautiful indeed. The photographer took a beautiful picture. Greg choked back tears as he thought more about it.

"I remember I was alone with Clarice," he said sadly.

Greg's memory of Clarice had deeply upset him. He was sad, sorrowful and gravely heartbroken. His sister, seeing her brother in such a distressed state, left him alone.

Greg slumped down in a swivel chair. He was tearful and broken-hearted. He mourned for Clarice. Greg stayed alone in the study. He had deep memories of Clarice. He remembered her at Tammy's party. He had been photographed together with Clarice by Tammy. To that very day, Greg had still never seen the photograph. The very last photograph taken by Tammy.

11

The Party Photograph

Greg was in his bedroom sitting down in an armchair, and reading a novel. This particular book belonged to a set for English Literature. Greg was disturbed by a knock on the door. He got up and answered his bedroom door. His sister came in and disturbed him from reading.

"Tammy is here. She's waiting downstairs," she said loudly.

"Thank you. I'll be down in a minute," replied Greg.

Greg applied aftershave. He rubbed it all over his neck. Greg groomed himself before going downstairs to meet Tammy, who was waiting alone in the lounge.

"I apologise I couldn't come sooner. I have been busy at work. Then there just wasn't time," explained Tammy.

"Have you brought the photo?" asked Greg.

"I have it," answered Tammy. She took many photos from her handbag and gave one to Greg. He looked at it with impatience.

Greg was heartbroken looking at the party photograph. Clarice and Greg were alone together.

They had posed together. It may have been the best photograph Tammy had taken at the party. It was a natural, friendly pose between Clarice and Greg. Greg spent some time looking at the photo, before giving it back to Tammy. He would never look at it again. He had only lasting memories of Clarice. He felt deeply sorrowful and pensive.

"Tammy, thank you," he said appreciatively.

"I do hope it's made a difference," gestured Tammy.

"It really has,"smiled Greg.

Tina entered the lounge, and both her and Tammy left together. They left the detached house, and headed for the car on the front drive. The passengers were awaiting departure to get back to work.

By himself, Greg got deeply upset again. He was mournful and deeply sad. He went back to his bedroom alone, where he stayed and mourned for Clarice. This time he wept for Clarice! Greg cried!

12

The Last Conversation of Clarice's Tragic Accident

Tammy came round to Tina's house (Tammy was responding in acknowledgement and response to Greg's request.) Greg expected Tammy to call at his house. They sat together in the living room and drank tea - except for Tammy who drank some still mineral water from a small bottle.

Tina kept silent as Greg conversed with Tammy, an American (a few of those whom Greg knew are unAmerican acquaintances.)

"Tell me, what sort of a person was Clarice?" asked Greg.

"Clarice was carefree, easy going and laid back, she loved children. She loved her horse. She loved classical music, literature, travelling and sightseeing. Clarice was a gourmet. So cultured. So intelligent and sophisticated. She was a good listener, and a good talker. Clarice loved riding. She liked to ride fast on her horse. Unfortunately she lost her life riding her horse. Her horse bolted. Clarice lost control and fell off. She died from a concussion."

"Oh, how awful! I thought she was a good rider," squinted Tina.

"Clarice was. Clarice was a reckless rider. She rode at breakneck speed,"responded Tammy.

They all mourned for Clarice. They had memories of Clarice at Tammy's party. This was the last time they had seen her alive. They deeply missed her, and were deeply saddened and mournful at their friend's loss to such a tragic riding accident.

"We will always remember Clarice, won't we? We must do something in remembrance of Clarice. Even if it's the last thing we ever do," said Tammy passionately.

As soon as their upsetting conversation had ended, Greg left Tammy alone with his sister. They both ended up talking about other things. Tina and Tammy recapped the discussion they had had last week.

Greg stayed in his bedroom alone and continued to read a book. Then he finished doing his homework for certain subjects, which had prolonged at not doing on time.

13

Greg's Opportunity Rose

Saturday evening, Greg sat waiting for his mother in the lounge. He was impatient at waiting. Within a quarter of an hour, his mother came into the lounge.

"Greg, come on! Let's get going!" said his mother impatiently.

Quickly, Greg and his mother left the house. They both walked to the car that was parked on the front drive. They both got into the motor car. Mrs Henning drove her son to Sara's cottage. Clarice's niece.

They reached the cottage. There Greg and his mother met Tammy, Tina and Sara. As soon as Greg and his mother arrived to pick up Tina, Sara, a little girl, started crying. She broke down.

"Don't cry," consoled Tammy. "Be strong. Remember Clarice. Do something for Clarice, in remembrance. In memory of Clarice."

Greg watched them. Greg got upset; Sara's deep emotion upset him. Tammy consoled and comforted Sara. Tammy rocked Sara like a child in her arms. Tammy held Sara passionately,

"We loved Clarice. We all did. Now, be strong for her. Make Clarice proud!" Tammy embraced Sara.

The others tried to console Sara, who was deeply sorrowful. Any and all comforting was ineffectual and unnecessary, as they were all unable to offer any comfort to Sara, who was deeply sad, and suffering from sorrow and bereavement.

"Sweetheart, take care. I must go, sweetie. You'll be alright," said Tina affectionately.

At Sara's home, Mrs Henning picked up a few passengers in her car to be driven home. She dropped two passengers home. One of them was staying at a friend's house for the night. Mrs Henning drove herself home, and was back within about half an hour.

A few hours later, Greg knocked on his sister's bedroom door.

"Come in," said his sister hoarsely.

Greg entered her bedroom, "I was wondering about Sara," he said. "She breaks my heart, is anyone taking care of her? She's vulnerable. She's in mourning. Who's going to look after her? Won't anyone help her?"

"You needn't worry," replied his sister. "Tammy is taking care of Sara. Tammy spends time with Sara, looking after her. Tammy babysits too."

Greg was reassured by Tina's assurance. He didn't worry about Sara anymore. Greg still showed deep concern for the sad, mournful child.

Greg left his sister's bedroom. He went into his bedroom, where he stayed for hours, reflecting on Sara;

a vulnerable child who was susceptible to being exposed, and from harm!

14

The Start of the Autumn Term

It was the first day back at secondary school. The beginning of the fourth year. In the hall, the pupils gathered together in their classes, waiting in the hall for their names to be called. All of the pupils were arranged into groups. Sets. from the top set, to the middle set, to the bottom set. Greg found himself in set two and set four. The bottom set for most of his groups. Greg had also chosen his options for alternative subjects. He had dropped certain subjects.

Greg compared himself to everybody else. He felt humiliated and embarrassed to be in the bottom set. Greg's bereavement had deeply affected him. During the school day he lacked concentration on anything else. Greg was stressed, anxious, and so lonely. He was labelled as a loner. He had been ignored and neglected by his form, and by everyone else in lessons and various classes.

Greg attended his first lessons of the day. His first lesson was double maths. His headteacher was the head of mathematics. One pupil in his maths lesson was a nuisance, a constant chatterbox. The headteacher preferred and favoured this schoolgirl, the chatterbox, more than anyone else in the class. In the class Greg did fractions and algebra. Starting this topic, he found it quite difficult. Greg hated maths.

After dinner time, Greg got back for registration. No one really took any notice or interest in Greg during the day. He was ignored and neglected by members of his own form. Even his form tutor neglected him, along with everybody else in the form.

After registration, Greg attended history (one of his option. He had dropped geography and foreign languages.) Greg learned about world history, including the second world war, from the outbreak of war to D-Day, to the liberation of Berlin by the Red Army, and the Nazi surrender.)

After Greg's history lesson, he went back to his form room. The form was dismissed. The pupils left their classroom and school to go home, either by coach, car or transport. Greg got home. In his bedroom he rested on his bed. He recovered from his tiredness. Later, he ate his evening meal in the dining room. He ate peas, mashed potatoes, and pie with gravy. Greg spent the rest of his time alone in his bedroom. He did no homework. He relaxed in his bedroom. He pondered on his first day back at school. He even reflected on Clarice. His last moments together with Clarice at Tammy's party. The very last photograph of the party taken by Tammy.

Greg ended up staying in his bedroom. He mourned for Clarice whom he had deeply loved, and was fond of. The stranger whom he had first met made him feel so sad and heartbroken, discovering Clarice had died in a tragic horse riding accident the following week.

Mrs Henning came into her son's bedroom and intruded on her son, "Are you doing your homework?" she asked. "I want you to work hard, not waste time."

"I am doing my homework. It's my first day back at school," explained Greg.

Tina was standing outside the bedroom door and overheard. She came in. Tina, a sympathiser, defended her brother,

"Mum, be reasonable. You should be sympathetic. My brother is in mourning."

"Tina, you have done well at school. I want my son to do well at school too."

Both mother and daughter left Greg alone. Greg was subdued as he spent more time grieving for Clarice.

15

Greg Spends Time With His Mournful Sister

One late night, Greg and Tina were in the lounge. They spent time together as soon as Tina had come home from her friend's house. They both had a conversation together. It was a personal conversation.

"How is Tammy?" asked Greg.

"Tammy is fine. She babysits and looks after Sara."

"How is Sara?"

Tina responded, speaking in a soft tone of voice, "Sara usually goes to bed early, but now she has late nights. She cries a lot. Sara is very sad. Her parents quarrel and argue. Tammy keeps the peace. Tammy takes care of Clarice's niece as best as she can under the circumstances. Tammy takes her shopping. Tammy buys Sara sweets. She reads her stories. Tammy plays with her, with her dolls. And they play boardgames. Tammy takes Sara to the park. Sara likes to see the swans, ducks and geese. Sara is at peace with nature. She's calm and peaceful in the park. Life won't get easy. Life will get hard. We have to try and cope with the loss of Clarice. We have to bring up Clarice's niece. We have to help and support Sara. Times are hard. But we have to cope with our troubles and problems. We have to overcome our suffering; our sadness and misery and difficulties. We have to get over it. It isn't easy. We have to do our best to get through it. Even though it's difficult and traumatic, our sorrow and bereavement."

"Sara needs love. Sara needs looking after. Sara shouldn't be neglected. She shouldn't be left alone," said Greg.

"I quite agree. Sara attends nursery. Also, her grandmother takes care of her and looks after her. I babysit when I can. I enjoy it. It's a pleasure to babysit; to take care of and look after Sara," replied his sister.

"It's really good that you look after Sara. you will be blessed doing that."

"I do what I can. It's such a tragedy to lose Clarice under these circumstances. I really loved her. I was fond of Clarice. Clarice was a friend of mine."

Greg sympathised with his sister, "Your time with Clarice was short. You had good times with Clarice."

"Oh I did! I certainly did. I had wonderful times with Clarice. I spent nights and days with Clarice. They were the best days that I spent with my friend."

Their emotional conversation ended. Both brother and sister simultaneously left the lounge together. They both went to bed so late on a Saturday night - about ten minutes to midnight.

Falling asleep, Greg dreamt. Greg had a sweet dream. He dreamt of a celestial paradise. He woke up later than usual in the morning. He couldn't remember his blissful dream. He had forgotten about his dream of paradise bliss (his rapture of the celestial heavens!) Did Clarice feature in his dream? He had no awareness of his subconsciousness. As Greg rose from his sleep, he still couldn't remember his blissful dream.

16

The Sad Times

Greg was alone in the garden. He walked around the garden. He admired the roses on the rose bushes. He smelled the natural scent of the roses. He saw the striking brilliance of all of the colours of the beautiful roses. The roses dazzled in the radiant sunshine. The wet roses sparkled from the raindrops running down the rose petals and rosebuds. Their conspicuousness was striking.

Greg stood and daydreamed while standing in the shadows. Greg was unaware that his sister's friends had come round. He wasn't expecting their arrival. Greg was engrossed in a daydream. His daydream preoccupied him.

Tina's friends waited in doors while she came outside into the garden. Tina disturbed her daydreaming brother, who was standing opposite the trees, lost in a reverie.

"Well, aren't you coming to meet my friends? They're here," said his sister.

"She's gone," whimpered Greg.

"Nothing can bring Clarice back. Come on! Meet my friends! They're waiting."

Tina put her hand on her brother's shoulder. She held him, moving him around until he stood and faced her. Both brother and sister were very sad, mournful and heartbroken over the tragic loss of Clarice. A rider who died in a horse riding accident (her horse had bolted and she had fallen off, dying as a result of her fall.)

Greg and Tina walked back to the house together. Going indoors, Greg met a few of Tina's friends. They were pleased to meet Greg, although he was bereaved, unconcerned and unexcited. Greg was intent on being alone. Seeking to have his own privacy to grieve for Clarice. However this opportunity arose, however fleeting, to meet Tina's friends. One of her friends, Jill, came forward and spoke in a soft voice,

"There you are. We wondered where you were."

"I was in the garden," said Greg.

Sandy patted Tina lightly on her back, "We've come to see our friend, but we came to see you too," she said to Greg.

"Oh, that's nice," Greg mumbled.

"I am sorry about Clarice. She was a dear friend of ours. We are all grieving. It must be deeply upsetting for you," continued Sandy lamentably.

Greg was tearful. He tried to suppress his tears, "It is. That cool stranger that was once with me at Tammy's party. I loved her. Why did it have to happen that way? Why did Clarice have to die? My time with

Clarice was short. I loved her very much, even though we were strangers when we first met."

Immediately, Tina and her friends left the room. Tina took a few of her friends upstairs to her bedroom. Tina wanted privacy with her friends. Greg, all alone, decided to stay downstairs in the lounge. He sat down in the armchair in the far corner of the room. He deeply mourned for Clarice. He was deeply concerned for Sara, Clarice's niece.

Greg deeply loved Clarice, a stranger. He pictured her dark eyes glinting in the firelight. Clarice's eyes were even prettier with eyeshadow, eyeliner and black mascara applied.

Suddenly Greg heard someone singing acapella from upstairs in his sister's bedroom. Then the tune changed. One of them sang for the church choir. A soprano. Jill had a very good voice. Sandy had a fairly good voice. And the other's voices were mediocre. This one was out of tune.

Greg thought that the choir singer was singing a lament. The following two sang as a duo. A sad song. A ballad. The sound of silence was disturbed by either a lament or a ballad. As Greg sat comfortably in the lounge chair, he felt tired and sleepy. He dozed off in the silence.

TWO DECADES LATER

17

The Secretary's Conduct

Tammy, the driver, was seated in her car. Sitting in the passenger seat beside her was Greg. Sara walked to the car, parked in a side street at a parking metre. Sara, a twenty-four-year-old, was relieved, unafraid and fearless. She was being given a lift home.

"Get me out of here," said Sara uneasily.

Sara, a leggy secretary, got into the back seat of the car. Tammy drove her back to her home in a rural village. The drive took less than three quarters of an hour. During the journey there were tailbacks and a diversion.

Once at Sara's home, Greg went upstairs with Sara. He admired the attractive secretary with long, shoulder-length hair cascading down her back. Sara resembled Clarice. There was a striking likeness.

"You really are something. You're quite a lady," said Greg.

"You were once a friend of Clarice, that means a lot to me. I do like to have you with me," smiled Sara.

"What was wrong back there?" asked Greg.

"I was being followed," answered Sara.

"Who by? Why didn't you say anything?"

"You know me. I may be crazy. I am quite unsure of myself."

"You're looking good," Greg complimented her.

"If you don't mind, I'd like to go to my room. I want to get some sleep."

Greg left Sara, the young secretary, alone. Her lacy bra and full breasts revealed through her see-through blouse.

Greg went downstairs alone and joined Tammy and Sara's mother, standing in the doorway. Tammy and Greg left the house. They both got in the car to go home. A few minutes earlier, Sara stood at the top bedroom window, overlooking the front drive. She had watched Tammy and Greg depart.

After afternoon tea, Greg and Tina remained seated on lounge chairs. Greg reclined. Tina confided in her brother,

"Sara says she was followed today. The person following her had gone when she got in the car."

"Hasn't Sara still got a mental illness? She's a disturbed young woman. It's no fault of her own. Why is her life so tragic?"

"Sara has problems. She finds it difficult to make friends and to have relationships," said Tina.

"Is Sara dating anyone?" asked Greg.

"No, Sara is single. Her boss makes advances."

"Oh, does he now?" said Greg in a sardonic tone of voice.

"Sara loves her job. She says it pays well. She tolerates her boss. She grovels for her job. She says it has its perks."

"How long can Sara keep it up for? How long will her job last for?" Greg wondered.

"I have thought about that. I've wondered if Sara's job will last," said Tina.

"Sara will do well. She is competitive and ambitious. She intends to be independent. A businesswoman."

"Well good luck to her I say!" exclaimed Tina deliriously.

"Sara is blessed. I am sure. Sara will make Clarice proud of her," said Greg proudly.

After their conversation ended, Greg and Tina got up from their chairs. They each pushed their chairs under the table. They left each other to go upstairs to their bedrooms. Greg ended up staying in his bedroom. For a long time he sat in his armchair. He mused on Sara, a difficult young woman who was possessed and disturbed. Sara was still bereaved as she grieved for Clarice.

18

The Weekend Visit

Greg, a volunteer, came from working at a charity shop in the highstreet. Tina, his sister, also came home from her job in the city. She was a secretary for a firm.

Greg sat down in an armchair. He relaxed sitting in the comfortable armchair. He was enervated and tired from working today (volunteering for a charitable organisation.)

Tina came into the lounge. Her beige raincoat slinky on her figure. She stood in front of her brother, who was drinking a cup of tea.

"Sara's got a boyfriend," she said.

Greg appeared to be unsurprised, "Sara needs talking to," he said disapprovingly.

"Sara is old enough. What she does is her own affair."

Greg disapproved of Sara having a boyfriend. He deemed it unwise for her to have one. He objected to Sara dating.

"Will Sara get married?" he asked.

"I don't know. She's not ready for it. She is in no fit state to get married."

"I quite agree. Sara shouldn't be dating and having relationships," said Greg.

"Knowing Sara, she'll ditch him. She just will. Why don't you come down this weekend? Sara will be bringing her boyfriend down," invited Tina.

"Is she? I could see her then. I am curious to see her boyfriend," replied Greg.

"Don't pass judgement until you meet him!" tutted Tina.

"Sara is mixed up. She needs a good talking to," said Greg unashamedly.

Greg raised his objection. Again, he disapproved of Sara having a boyfriend.

Tina left the room, and Greg thought of Sara for a short time. He did not dwell on it any further. Greg was disgusted. It caused him disgust.

Greg was protective of Sara. He protected her the same way Tammy did. Tammy was once a good friend to Clarice. Leaving the lounge, Greg went to his bedroom. He spent the night reading a novel. A literary work by a great author.

19

Greg Checks Out Sara's Beau

Greg drove to Sara's house. He wanted to know what her beau was like. He disapproved of Sara having a relationship. A romance.

He got out of his car. He locked the car door. He walked up to the house and to the front door. He pressed the doorbell. It made a chiming sound.

Greg was unenthusiastic about going there that night. But he was eager to know what sort of a person Sara's boyfriend was. He had discouraged Sara from having a boyfriend. He told her about having priorities. He emphasised the most important priority, which is of essential importance.

Instead, Sara had pleased herself and done what she desired.

Entering the detached house, Greg met Sara's boyfriend for the first time. They had been dating each other since the conference. Sara, a secretary, had attended the meeting in the conference room, and was assigned to take the minutes.

Greg firmly shook the businessman's hand. His first impression of the handsome businessman was that he was articulate, eloquent and an intellectual. He envied the charming gentleman who was doing his best to make an admirable impression.

Sara's parents approved of Mr Stent. They both seemed to like him. Greg was tired from concentrating on the drive. He decided to keep away from everyone as he was moody and short tempered. He felt unwelcome at first.

Greg felt he had outstayed his welcome. He left minutes later to avoid all those concerned. He had to find out about Sara's boyfriend; whether he was admirable, desirable, and suitable for her. Was Mr Stent unsuitable?

Greg said goodbye to everyone in a hurry. He was impatient to get out and go. Greg left the house and went to his car. It was the very last car parked on the drive. He opened the car door. He got in his car. He reversed his car out of the drive. He steered the wheel as he drove the car out onto the pitch dark road. The road was endlessly long. Greg drove back home.

There was no one else at home in the dark house. The skies were sapphire-black. The night was pitch-black with street lights shining in the mist. In the misty night.

Sara's family members all shared different opinions. Some of them wanted Sara to be married, and others wanted her to remain unmarried - a spinster. There was a difference of opinion.

In the end, Sara remained unmarried. It was Clarice's wish, and Sara's mother's too. The family did approve of Sara's beau. He was a likeable young businessman. A materialist. A chauvinist with ambition. Mr Stent desired to get married. It remains his wish.

Sara remains a spinster!

Available worldwide from Amazon
and all good bookstores

Michael Terence
Publishing

www.mtp.agency

www.facebook.com/mtp.agency

@mtp_agency

www.ingramcontent.com/pod-product-compliance
Ingram Content Group UK Ltd.
Pitfield, Milton Keynes, MK11 3LW, UK
UKHW031825150325
456310UK00001B/29